Investigations of

The Reverend Lyle Thorne

Mysteries from the Golden Age of Detection

Ray Moore

This book is a work of fiction. Names, characters, places, and incidents either are the product of the author's imagination or are used fictitiously and any resemblance to actual persons, living or dead, business establishments, events or locales is entirely coincidental.

Dedication

This book is for my wife Barbara because she loves mystery and crime fiction and encouraged me to write these stories.

Contents

Preface

He was my friend, faithful and just to me.
(William Shakespeare, *Julius Caesar*)

Chief Inspector Frederick George Abberline of
Scotland Yard did not always enjoy an easy working
relationship with Detective Sergeant Lyle Thorne.
Abberline considered that Thorne, who was still in his
mid-twenties, had been promoted far too young, and
that, as a result, he was arrogant, impulsive,
unorthodox, insubordinate, brilliant, and (far too
often) right. Perhaps this explains why, early in
September 1888, when the then Inspector First-Class
Frederick George Abberline was seconded to
Whitechapel H Division in order to coordinate the
police investigations into the murders of prostitutes
Emma Elizabeth Smith, Martha Tabram, and Mary
Ann Nichols, he had specifically requested the
assistance of Lyle Thorne. The story of the notorious
Whitechapel Murders is too familiar to require
repeating, but one hitherto unrecorded consequence
of that investigation, and specifically of its failure to
discover the identity of the murderer, was that, in
March 1889, Detective Sergeant Lyle Thorne
resigned from the Metropolitan Police. In his
posthumously published memoirs, Abberline stated
unequivocally of Thorne that "he was at once the
most difficult and the most able detective with whom
I ever had the honor of serving."

None of this was known to me when I first met
The Reverend Lyle Thorne in January, 1910. As a
newly ordained curate fresh out of Theological

i

College, I had been appointed to the parish of Sanditon*, a small resort town on the South Coast which was, in the decade before The Great War, becoming quite popular with those visitors who professed to find towns such as Brighton and Bournemouth too large and vulgar. Thorne was then in his mid-forties and was an imposing (not to say intimidating) figure. Standing six feet two inches tall, with close-cropped iron-grey hair, he tended to dominate any company he was in not so much because of his sheer size as because of his calm air of self-assurance. Only gradually over the four years of our professional association did I earn his confidence and come to learn the truth about the past of Lyle Thorne. These narratives document that process, as well as illustrating precisely why Inspector Abberline had held Lyle Thorne in such high regard

It was only on my last day as curate at Sanditon that I finally summoned the courage to ask my mentor and friend why he had resigned from the Metropolitan Police at a time when he had a growing reputation and an assured future in the force. He informed me that he had been one of the first detectives on the scene when the body of Mary Jane Kelly, generally believed to have been the last victim of the serial killer who the world came to know as Jack the Ripper, was discovered.

"Kelly was the youngest victim," he told me, "and, by all accounts, had been an attractive woman. When I saw her, however, her body had been hideously mutilated. It was a terrible sight that I have never been able to forget. This was not just crime, Knowles: I felt that I had been brought face-to-face with pure evil. My calling to the Church dated from that moment."

Thorne served as vicar of the South Coast resort of Sanditon from 1906 until his retirement in 1927. However, if Thorne had anticipated a quiet, uneventful life at Sanditon vicarage, he was to be disappointed, for his reputation as an investigator attracted a succession of 'clients' each with a remarkable tale.

My four years as Rev. Thorne's curate were the foundation of a life-long friendship which only ended when Rev. Lyle Thorne died in 1948 at the age of eighty-seven.

Reginald Knowles

October 1951

* Readers may notice that I have borrowed this name from the work of Miss Jane Austen. Like the fictional Sanditon, the town which Lyle Thorne served as vicar for two decades owed its development in the 1790's to the fashion for sea bathing. During this time, speculative builders erected Waterloo Crescent, meeting rooms, and a theater in imitation of Bath and Cheltenham. Sadly, by the time the town was ready to become fashionable, the fashion for sea bathing had passed, and it never rivaled the larger resort towns of the South Coast. Readers may take this digression as fair notice that certain other details in these narratives (dates, names, etc.) have also been fictionalized to protect the privacy of those involved in these investigations and of their descendants.

The Case of the Fallen Woman
September 1911

Thou hast committed –
Fornication: but that was in another country
And besides, the wench is dead.
(Christopher Marlowe, *The Jew of Malta*)

Early morning sunlight slanted through the leaded dining room windows of the vicarage where Rev. Lyle Thorne and I had just completed a leisurely breakfast. For the previous five days, Thorne had been suffering the effects of a severe case of food poisoning which had its origin in a sack of questionable oysters which he had unwisely purchased from the local market, so I had, with the greatest of difficulty, prevailed upon him to delegate to me all of his parish duties. For the first time since his appointment to the parish of Sanditon in 1906, Rev. Thorne had taken something approaching a rest.

I confess to feeling a certain self-satisfaction with Thorne's restored health and vigor, and I was preparing to pronounce him entirely recovered and to suggest that he begin work on his next sermon when a knocking at the door disturbed my complacency.

Our housekeeper, Elizabeth, entered the dining room and handed Thorne a note which he read with evident interest. He looked up from the note, which he pushed towards me. That note was the first indication I had of Rev. Lyle Thorne's former profession. Looking across the breakfast table, I saw an unaccustomed, mischievous look in his eye which gave me some vague cause for concern.

"Well Knowles," he began, "your confidence in the completeness of my recovery may be tested rather sooner than you might have wished. Our Inspector Campbell appears to believe that I may be able to assist him in an investigation which he has on hand." He turned to the housekeeper and continued, "Please show the Inspector in, Elizabeth."

"Thorne," I began reprovingly, "you surely are not well enough to…"

My protest was silenced by Thorne's raised right hand, a gesture which I already recognized as final. Elizabeth showed into the room a man in his early thirties who strode purposefully towards my friend with outstretched hand.

"Inspector Campbell," said Thorne rising to shake the policeman's hand, "allow me to introduce my young curate Reginald Knowles. Please, help yourself to some of this excellent tea – you will find a cup on the sideboard – and take a seat." Thorne paused to give our visitor time to pour himself some tea and to make himself comfortable in an armchair before he continued, "And now, Inspector, to what, may I ask, do I owe this unexpected pleasure?"

"First, Rev. Thorne, I must ask you to please forgive me for intruding on you like this. I know that since you came to Sanditon you have not made public your former connection with the Metropolitan Police, though it is, of course, a matter of official record. I myself served at Scotland Yard before I was transferred to Sanditon, and I can assure you that they still talk of your cases there. To be quite frank, sir, I need your help. It's this way…"

The Case of the Fallen Woman

Inspector Campbell broke off and appeared to be gathering his thoughts; this was clearly not a social call. Before he proceeded with his narrative, he took from the pocket of his Norfolk jacket a small notebook which he consulted repeatedly.

"We... that is I... discovered a body this morning at the foot of the cliffs. A lady was reported missing last night. Her husband reported it at 9.00 p.m. He and his wife were staying at The Drovers... had been since midday Monday... So, of course, I went to talk to him immediately, though I was pretty confident that by the time I got to The Drovers, his wife would have returned.

"Well, I was wrong: she hadn't, but it being already pretty near to dark, there wasn't much I could do. Oh, I searched the cliff walk with a lamp which I borrowed from the hotel, but there being no moon to speak of, I wasn't at all surprised to find no trace of the lady. Leaving word at The Drovers that I was to be contacted first thing in the morning if the lady had not returned, I made my way back to the station house.

"Anyway, young Freddie Marsh, the day porter at The Drovers, called me by telephone at about 6 a.m. this morning to tell me that the woman had not returned during the night, so I began a thorough search of the cliff walk and saw her body at about 6.20 a.m. It was at a spot where the cliff walk comes dangerously close to the edge of the cliff - not more than a few feet since that storm last winter caused a fresh rock fall. It was immediately clear that the lady had fallen, and that she was beyond helping. Examining the ground on the path, I found only one set of footprints, and from the look of them I concluded that the lady seemed to have stumbled and lost her footing. From where she fell it's seventy feet or more onto jagged rocks.

"It took me some time to make my way down to the beach, and there the body of the lady was, lying on a ledge of rock several feet above the highest tide mark, so the sea hadn't touched her." The Inspector, speaking with evident difficulty, paused. "I don't mind telling you, Rev. Thorne, that it has fair shaken me. She must have been a very attractive young woman when alive, but the fall from the cliff had left her terribly... damaged... terribly."

Inspector Campbell's halting narrative came to an end.

"How awful!" I heard myself remark, realizing at once how woefully inadequate was my response. "But, if you do not mind my asking Inspector, how do you need the Vicar's help with the investigation of what appears to be a tragic case of accidental death?"

"Well, Mr. Knowles, no doubt you are right, but still I would value Rev. Thorne's opinion," Inspector Campbell explained, gradually recovering his composure. "To be honest with you, this is the first death which I have investigated since I was promoted to the rank of inspector and transferred to Sanditon. I should hate to have overlooked anything. There *is* something about this matter that troubles me, but I cannot for the life of me say what it is. If you could both accompany me when I talk with the husband, Mr. Brownloe, I should be much obliged. Poor man, he's extremely upset, of course... especially with having to identify the body this morning and all. I'm sure he'd appreciate the involvement of a man of your standing. And then, Rev. Thorne, if you would be kind enough to examine the scene of the accident, just to make sure, I should feel easier in my mind. You see, your reputation for gathering evidence which eludes other members of the police service has gone before you. The body had to be removed, of course, but I have four constables posted to make sure that nothing else is disturbed."

I could see at once that Thorne's interest, and perhaps also his vanity, had been aroused.

"Yes, of course, Inspector," he said. "I will do anything I can to help."

I was about to object when Thorne anticipated me, "Now Knowles, do not fuss. You have taken excellent care of me for four days, and I am now quite recovered and craving some intellectual stimulation. Where is Mr. Brownloe now, Inspector?"

"He's at The Drovers, Vicar, resting in his room. I had Dr. Millington take a look at him. Millington declared Mrs. Brownloe dead - though there wasn't any doubt about it, poor woman! I asked the doctor to remain whilst her husband identified the body because the gentleman suffers from asthma, and I feared that the shock might bring on another attack. Mr. Brownloe had been unwell the previous evening which is why he didn't accompany his wife on her evening walk. If he had, then this would never have happened."

"Knowles and I will walk straight over with you Inspector," Thorne stated rising from the table and calling to Elizabeth for our jackets. "Where is Mrs. Brownloe's body?"

"Taken to the local hospital. Dr. Millington saw to the arrangements. There will have to be an inquest, of course, but in this case it'll only be a formality. That cliff walk has been a danger for months. I've warned the Parish Council about it time and again!" There was real bitterness in the Inspector's voice.

Together the three of us walked down to the seafront promenade, now sparsely populated by late-season visitors, in the pure sunlight of the September morning. It seemed to me outrageous that death should come (and in such a hideous form) on such a beautiful day. Reaching the driveway of The Drovers, I paused to look up to the summit of the white cliffs rising high above the bay to the west of the town trying, without success, to find some indication of the exact spot where the tragedy had taken place.

Entering the lobby, Inspector Campbell introduced us to Frederick Marsh who was at the reception desk and asked him if Mr. Brownloe was still in his room. Marsh confirmed that he was and then turned to address Thorne.

"Shocking business, Rev. Thorne... horrible," he began. "Millie's quite upset. She talked with Mrs. Brownloe, you see, just before the lady went out for her evening walk yesterday. Millie seemed quite taken with her."

Inspector Campbell quietly explained to me that Millicent Haver, who worked at The Drovers as a maid, was Frederick Marsh's fiancée.

"Tell me about Mr. and Mrs. Brownloe," Thorne asked the porter. "It will help me to know something about them before I see the grieving husband."

The Case of the Fallen Woman

"There's little enough to tell, Vicar," Marsh began. "I was on duty on Monday afternoon. You can see from the hotel register that they arrived at about two in the afternoon. He signed the register and gave an address in London. The reservation had been confirmed by letter the previous week, so everything was in order. Here is the letter." He slid the paper across the desk, but Thorne merely glanced at it. "They intended staying until Thursday morning. Mr. Brownloe is in his early forties, but she was younger - mid-twenties I'd say, though Millie thought a little older. They took two adjoining rooms with a sea view and a shared sitting room, which is what he had requested in his letter, as you can see."

Marsh pushed the hotel register towards Thorne who examined it briefly, and then the day porter continued his account:

"When I came on duty this morning, the night porter told me, as I said, that Mrs. Brownloe had failed to return from her evening walk and that Inspector Campbell had asked to be notified, so I called him on the telephone. Apparently, Mr. Brownloe had been out searching several times during the night, but had finally returned to his rooms in a state of nervous exhaustion (he suffers from asthma, I understand) and was at that time asleep. Well, as I said, I telephoned the Inspector immediately and confirmed that the lady was still missing. The Inspector told me that he intended to conduct a thorough search, and later he came to tell Mr. Brownloe that a body had been found. That would be about 7.00 a.m. or a little before. About two hours later, Dr. Millington brought Mr. Brownloe back to his room after he had identified his wife's body at the local hospital. He left him there in the care of his secretary, I understand."

"No one has mentioned a secretary before," Thorne remarked sharply. "When did he arrive?"

"*She,* Vicar," Frederick corrected, "arrived yesterday afternoon a few hours after Mr. and Mrs. Brownloe. The lady came up to the desk at about 5 p.m. I remember the time because I was just making preparations to go home. She asked if Mr. Brownloe had taken rooms. I told the lady that Mr. Brownloe and his wife were staying at the hotel, and she explained that she was the gentleman's secretary. Some unexpected business had come up - papers, which urgently needed his signature - so she had caught the next train to Sanditon. She'd known his destination apparently, but not the name of the hotel where he and his wife intended to stay.

"Anyway, the lady booked herself a small room. You can see her name in the register: Miss Susan Phillips. She told me that she would only stay for a single night because she intended to return to London early the next day with the signed papers. Then she wrote a short note to her employer and asked me if I could see that he got the note without Mrs. Brownloe being disturbed - apparently Mrs. Brownloe was very sensitive about business affairs interrupting a holiday. A few minutes after I had shown her to her room, Mr. Brownloe happened to be walking alone through the lobby, so I put the note directly into his hand. He told me that his wife was resting in their rooms. Shortly after that, I went home for the evening."

The Case of the Fallen Woman

I was still trying to digest everything that Inspector Campbell and Freddie Marsh had said as we three climbed the elegant winding staircase of The Drovers to the second floor rooms which Mr. Brownloe occupied, but I was not too caught up in my own thoughts that I did not notice the new energy in Thorne's stride and the look of intense concentration on his face. On the landing, Thorne pulled me aside briefly.

"Deep waters, my friend. I begin to share the Inspector's intuition about this case. Perhaps, very deep waters indeed," he whispered with an excitement in his voice which I had never noticed the Scriptures to generate. We continued up the stairs.

Eventually reaching the door of the sitting room, the Inspector knocked quietly, and the door was opened almost immediately by an elegant lady in her late thirties whose face must normally have been quite beautiful for a woman of her age, though now it betrayed signs of considerable strain.

"Excuse me, madam," Inspector Campbell began. "You will remember me from this morning, and this is The Rev. Lyle Thorne and his curate, Mr. Knowles. We have called to speak with Mr. Brownloe."

"Yes, of course, Inspector," the lady replied in a deliberately quiet voice. "Do come in. Mr. Brownloe is still sleeping in his room; the doctor gave him a mild sedative. I will wake him in a moment, but might I have a word with you first?"

"We are entirely at your disposal, madam," Campbell politely replied.

"Firstly, I should introduce myself properly. I am Mr. Brownloe's private secretary, Miss Phillips. It is merely by chance that I am here at all. Mr. Brownloe neglected to sign some contracts so I came to Sanditon yesterday. They seemed so important at the time, but now..."

The sentence hung in the air unfinished, and tears, which the lady had been holding back, began to flow silently.

"Pray do not distress yourself," I said, placing what I hoped would be a comforting hand on the woman's arm, and directing her toward the sofa.

"Thank you, Mr. Knowles. I am afraid it has all been too much of a shock to me, but it was of Mr. Brownloe that I wanted to speak. He really is a good man." The lady said this with an emphasis which almost implied that someone had denied it. "And a good husband, though unfortunately there are no children - something which I know caused his wife great sorrow. He seems particularly to want the body of Mrs. Brownloe to be buried in the Sanditon parish churchyard. Will that be possible?"

"I can see no reason why not," Inspector Campbell replied. "There will be all of the legal formalities, of course, but I do not anticipate any problems there. Do you have any objection, Vicar?"

Rev. Thorne replied that he would be willing to make the necessary arrangements and, if requested, to conduct the funeral service as soon as the body had been released by the coroner.

"I am so glad," Miss Phillips said with an audible sigh. "It will be a comfort to Mr. Brownloe. I will inform him that you are here."

So saying, Miss Phillips went to the bedroom, knocked quietly on the door and immediately entered, leaving us alone in the sitting room which, I noticed for the first time, offered a magnificent view of the western side of the bay. Moving to the window, Inspector Campbell identified for Thorne and myself the precise section of the cliff walk from which Mrs. Brownloe had fallen to her death.

Our observations were interrupted when the door to the bedroom opened. Mr. Brownloe was of medium height with slightly receding brown hair streaked with gray and the beginnings of a double-chin. With these exceptions, he retained the athletic build and posture of a much younger man, and I felt that, under normal circumstances, he would have appeared handsome. Now, however, his face looked drawn and haggard, and his beautifully tailored suit, in which he had quite obviously slept, was extremely creased. Almost timidly, he extended a hand to my friend.

"I cannot thank you enough for coming, Rev. Thorne. Inspector Campbell promised this morning that he would talk with you about what has happened. Miss Phillips has informed me that you and she have spoken about the funeral arrangements. I am glad because I am not sure that I am capable of making too much sense. I have asked Miss Phillips to order some tea. It seems almost wicked to acknowledge it, but I have had nothing either to eat or drink since before I arrived here yesterday afternoon, and I really feel in need of it."

"Perfectly understandable, Mr. Brownloe," I replied. "May I express my profound sympathy for the death of your wife? If there is anything I can do..." Once again, the inadequacy of my words to the occasion struck me.

"Thank you, young man. It has been a profound shock. However, it is a great comfort to me to know that my wife's wishes will be respected. I know that she would have wanted to be buried here in Sanditon. It was a part of the country that she loved, and only yesterday, as we were being driven from the railway station, she particularly remarked on the beauty of your Regency church. It is where she would have chosen to rest."

Inspector Campbell explained that he saw no objection to the proposal, though he did urge Mr. Brownloe to give it some longer consideration and enquired as to the wishes of his wife's family.

"Mrs. Brownloe has no immediate family," he replied almost curtly. "Her parents are both dead, she is an only-child, and... and there are no children. I really think that her wishes, and my own, should be sufficient in this case." It was the first time in our conversation that the strain which he was under had revealed itself in the man's tone.

Fortunately, the tension in the room was broken at that moment by a knock at the door and a maid entering with a tray containing tea and sandwiches. She was followed by Miss Phillips. The maid quickly withdrew, and Miss Phillips was about to do the same when Mr. Brownloe asked her to stay. She began to pour the tea.

Inspector Campbell seemed reluctant to ask questions of the grieving husband, and as a result conversation was not easy. Mr. Brownloe explained the business which had brought his secretary to

Sanditon and proposed that (providing Inspector Campbell had no objection) Miss Phillips should return to London later that afternoon. There were certain contracts, now signed which, he insisted, it was imperative to deliver. Mr. Brownloe stated that he would himself remain at The Drovers until the funeral.

When our limping conversation finally came to a halt, Thorne and I found an appropriate opportunity to take our leave of the others, Thorne assuring Mr. Brownloe that he would be in contact with him as soon as he had any definite information.

Thorne contrived that he and I should leave The Drovers without encountering anyone by taking a narrow, little-used staircase which led via a corridor to a rear door. When I asked Thorne how he had found this exit, which appeared to date from the time when the hotel had been a private house and to have hardly been used since that time, he replied simply, "Because I was looking for it, Knowles."

Thorne walked silently, deep in his own thoughts, and I already knew better than to interrupt him. At the end of the almost deserted promenade, we descended the stone steps onto the shingle beach and were soon approaching the place where the body had been discovered, though it had, as Inspector Campbell had informed us, been removed several hours previously. The shingle gave way to stones as we climbed higher up the beach, and finally we had to clamber over boulders and fallen rock to get to the area beneath the limestone cliffs where the body of Mrs. Brownloe had been found. Two constables were stationed there to keep away mawkish sensation-seekers, but when Thorne approached both saluted briskly and allowed him through.

There were no obvious signs of the tragedy: nature had been left to begin the process of eradicating any marks of the horror which had happened there. Minute inspection of the rocks above the high tide mark, however, gave Thorne a clear indication of precisely where Mrs. Brownloe's body had lain following her fall. It had come to rest only a few feet from the foot of the cliff, suggesting that there had been no great momentum in the fall from the cliff top such as might have been produced by a deliberate jump. In my own mind, I ruled out suicide.

Thorne spent fully half an hour examining the rocks where the body had fallen, using his powerful magnifying glass to look over every inch. Aware that I could be of no assistance to my friend, except by ensuring that he suffered no interruption, I had walked away from the foot of the cliffs and finally had sat down on a ledge of rock about twenty-five yards from where Thorne was conducting his minute examination. It was there that I noticed, almost between my feet, a boulder about the size of my fist which was significantly larger that the surrounding stones lying where the in-coming tide threatened soon to have enveloped it. Without precisely knowing why, I bent forward and picked it up. Close examination of its surface revealed minute signs of blood and skin, and a single, long strand of human hair.

"Thorne!" I called excitedly. "Look at this."

At first, Thorne gave an exclamation of impatience, but upon looking at the boulder with his lens, his attitude markedly changed.

"Knowles, you appear to have missed your vocation!" he exclaimed. "Thanks to you, I believe that it remains only for me to resolve one or two minor elements of this crime which are still unclear to me, and then I trust that we can leave the details to the good Inspector."

"Crime, Thorne!" I exclaimed. "But I thought that the poor woman was the victim of a terrible accident."

"Murder, my dear Knowles," Thorne replied, "as the rock which you discovered proves beyond doubt." I clearly must have looked as puzzled as I felt, because my friend explained, "Trajectory, Knowles. Remember your physics - Newton's Second Law of Motion: Force is equal to mass times acceleration." Since this clearly added nothing to my understanding of the significance of the evidence which I had found, my friend offered an explanation in the simplest terms:

"Had this rock simply been dislodged during the fall, it would have fallen close to the body, but in fact it was fully twenty yards nearer to the sea. What do you conclude from that, Knowles?"

"Good Lord Thorne!" I shouted. "The rock was thrown *at* Mrs. Brownloe. It is the murder weapon!"

"Quite," Thorne confirmed in a somewhat patronizing tone.

It took twenty minutes of hard walking for us to reach the point on the cliff walk from which Mrs. Brownloe had fallen. Here again we found two constables guarding the area from the eyes of the curious, but as below when they saw Thorne approach each gave a salute and moved aside.

"If we are correct, Knowles," Thorne said, "we should expect to find only a single set of footprints on the path, and nothing which might have caused the victim to stumble or lose her footing – loose rocks or a protruding root, for example. Please examine the cliff walk (without stepping on it) whilst I take a look over here."

The cliff walk was well used in summer, but the season being late fewer people ventured upon it. One set of recent footprints was indeed evident, and I saw clearly where they ended. Just as Inspector Campbell had reported, the prints indicated a sudden loss of balance and disappeared from the path. I reported my findings to Thorne.

"I assumed that Campbell had read the signs correctly, the man seems to me to be quite competent – still, it is best to check. I believe that our murderer stood behind those bushes," he said pointing to a clump of vegetation about ten yards away. "The ground is newly disturbed, though since the soil is compacted there are, unfortunately, no clear footprints." Thorne paused before he added, "And now, I believe that we just have to question Miss Haver, and then, I fancy, I might turn my attention back to those duties for which the Church of England pays me an annual stipend, and which the Archbishop of Canterbury (whom I have in reality never met) is under the mistaken impression that I actually discharge."

The Case of the Fallen Woman

Millicent Haver proved to be a beautiful young woman of around twenty. We found her that evening in the cottage where she lived with her mother and two sisters. I have often remarked that Lyle Thorne who, being devoutly celibate, had no interest whatsoever in the fairer sex, nevertheless had a way of recommending himself to women, and so it was on this occasion. The three of us set out on a walk to the headland, which is on the east side of the bay away from the cliffs which Thorne knew that Miss Haver had every reason to wish to avoid.

"Millie," Thorne began speaking in a calm, reassuring tone, "I saw Freddie today, and he told me how upset you were by Mrs. Brownloe's death. Now, I don't want to upset you further, but I should really like to know something more about her. Freddie said that you were quite taken with the lady."

"Oh Vicar, it would be a relief to talk about it to someone. It has made me miserable all day," Millie said. "Well, let me see. It was just a little after seven yesterday evening. I was carrying some cutlery to the dining room when Mrs. Brownloe stopped me. Oh, she was a lovely lady, sir, and I don't mean just to look at, though she was what most men would call beautiful. She asked me my name and how long I had worked at the Drovers. We had a proper little conversation before cook told to me in no uncertain terms to get a move on. Not stuck-up like some of the people we have here she wasn't! As she went out of the door, she asked directions to the cliff walk. Oh, Rev. Thorne, I did warn her not to go too close to the edge of the cliff, and she called back as she was going out of the front door that she would take great care. And that... that is the last time I saw her."

Millie wept silently into a small white handkerchief.

"What happened after that Millie?" Thorne asked in a gentle, coaxing voice.

"Well, the next thing I heard was that Mr. Brownloe was taken very ill, so the porter had gone to Miss Phillips' room and asked her to go to his rooms since his wife was not in the hotel. There was some talk of sending for Dr. Millington, but Miss Phillips insisted that Mr. Brownloe quite often had attacks of asthma and that he carried his own medication. Miss Phillips stayed with Mr. Brownloe in his room waiting for his wife's return. Mr. and Mrs. Brownloe were due to have supper in their room at half past eight, so they didn't anticipate having to wait long. The night porter says it was Miss Phillips who came to the desk to report Mr. Brownloe's growing concern for his wife's safety and to insist that the police be notified."

Eventually, Millie became calmer, and then Thorne ventured a further question, "Millie, have you met Miss Susan Phillips?"

"Not to speak to, I haven't, though I've seen her once or twice. Everyone seems to think her very attentive to Mr. Brownloe," Millie replied in a tone which clearly hinted that she had formed no positive impression of the lady secretary.

"Think very carefully, Millie," Thorne said speaking slowly and deliberately. "When Miss Phillips went to Mr. Brownloe's room because of his asthma attack, did she stay there the whole time that Mrs. Brownloe was away?"

"I really can't say Vicar. I was working in the dining room, as I told you, setting up for breakfast, and then, of course, I went home. It was my impression that she did... certainly I didn't see her again and neither did anyone else that I've spoken to."

We walked Millie back to her cottage, and Thorne and I then began our slow stroll back to the vicarage. On the way, Rev. Thorne set out the facts of the case, speaking rather to himself than to me:

"Mrs. Brownloe was murdered – it is as straightforward a case of murder as I have ever encountered – sometime between 7.00 p.m. when she left The Drovers to take her walk and 8.30 p.m. when she would have needed to have returned to the hotel in time for supper. That much is perfectly clear. During most of this period, Brownloe and Miss Phillips were apparently together in his rooms as a result of his sudden illness, but at some point Miss Philips left The Drovers without being seen. We have ourselves proved that that would be no great matter. I am convinced that Brownloe's indisposition was genuine, though as to the cause, I can only speculate. I suggest that the content of the note which Miss Phillips sent him would tell us that, but I am quite sure that it has been destroyed for that very reason. Unfortunately, there is nothing here, Knowles, that Inspector Campbell would call evidence, and jury would call it all circumstantial and dismiss the case out of hand. Mr. Brownloe and Miss Phillips will, I am convinced, give each other an absolute alibi, which I shall be unable to break unless I could find someone who saw Miss Phillips leave The Drovers or saw her on the cliff walk that night, and since no such witness has come forward so far, that seems to me to be most unlikely."

As the last few days of September passed, I made discrete enquiries of Dr. Millington who confirmed that Mr. Brownloe's asthmatic condition was indeed genuine. Thorne's extensive questioning at The Drovers and in the surrounding area failed to locate anyone who had seen Miss Phillips leave Mr. Brownloe's rooms after she had entered them. No one had seen either Mrs. Brownloe or Miss Phillips on the cliff walk that evening. If Miss Phillips had slipped out of The Drovers, no one had seen her leave, and no one had seen her return. An Inquest was promptly held and duly brought in a finding of death by misadventure. The body was released for burial.

The afternoon of the funeral was cold and overcast, punctuated by sharp showers. Only a small number of people attended the burial service: Inspector Campbell, Dr. Millington, Millie leaning heavily on Frederick for support, the manager and some other staff from The Drovers. Mr. Brownloe had remained in Sanditon since his wife's death; Miss Phillips had returned that day to attend the service. There were no family members. The small congregation occupied only the first three rows of the imposing Regency church.

The Vicar of Sanditon, speaking about a woman whom he had never met, recounted (at second hand) that she had been a faithful and loyal wife, and that she had supported her husband in his business career. He also commented approvingly on the positive impression she had made on those who had met her. In conclusion, he urged that, even when faced with apparently inexplicable tragedy, it is not for man to question the ways of God.

As he spoke, I noticed Rev. Thorne staring intently from the pulpit towards Mr. Brownloe and Miss Phillips who were sitting together in the front pew. That lady, dressed in a fashionable black wool suit, sat with her head bowed, dabbing her eyes with a spotless lace handkerchief, but I noticed that Mr. Brownloe's eyes kept coming back to Thorne.

After the brief service, the small, melancholy group followed the coffin to the graveside, and Mrs. Brownloe was laid to rest. Thorne drew me towards the church gate where we stood awaiting the mourners as they began to drift away. Finally, Mr. Brownloe approached leading Miss Phillips on his arm. They were accompanied by Inspector Campbell.

"Goodbye Rev. Thorne. Goodbye Knowles," the Inspector said shaking out hands in turn. "I cannot tell you how much easier I feel having had your help in this matter."

Miss Susan Phillips approached holding out her hand first to Thorne and then to me. I did not see that I had any option but to take it.

"She was a fine woman, and it was terrible that she died in that way," the lady said in a strained voice.

"Will you return to London today, sir?" Rev. Thorne inquired of Mr. Brownloe.

"Indeed," he replied with a heavy sigh. "I fear that I must take up the running of my business once again."

Mr. Brownloe thanked Rev. Thorne, and then he and Miss Phillips turned together and walked slowly, arm-in-arm towards a waiting cab.

"Mrs. Brownloe!" Rev. Thorne called suddenly in a booming, commanding voice.

The lady at Mr. Brownloe's side, his private secretary, turned her head and her upper body the merest fraction of an inch before she brought the instinctive movement under firm control. But, it was enough – and all five of us knew that it was enough. We stood, as though frozen in time, looking at each other - for a moment sharing the whole terrible truth.

Inspector Campbell was the first of us to move. He turned towards Thorne with a look of utter astonishment.

"I believe," Thorne began, "that we may now safely leave the remainder of this investigation in your hands, Inspector?"

"I assure you that you can do so with complete confidence, sir," Campbell replied moving purposefully towards Mr. Brownloe and his female companion. He added, speaking very deliberately, "My thanks to you, detective sergeant."

When we were finally alone in the churchyard, Rev. Thorne said, in a voice which contained more than a hint of nostalgia, "I think, Knowles, that there is something to be said for a little extra intellectual stimulation in the quiet life of a clergyman after all.

The Case of the Anonymous Cleric
April 1912

> For the great majority of mankind are satisfied
> with appearance, as though they were realities and
> are often more influenced by the things that seem
> than by those that are.
> (Nicolo Machiavelli, *The Prince*)

The elderly gentleman seated one late afternoon in
the deep armchair opposite The Rev. Lyle Thorne
appeared to me like a grotesque character who had
stepped out of the pages of one of Mr. Dickens'
earlier novels. He was a clergyman of the Roman
Catholic persuasion, and he apparently took his
calling seriously for in his left hand he held a small
Bible bound in red leather. The clerical smock which
he wore had seen better days, and the long, flax-like
hair which emerged from under his hat fell, dull and
lifeless, upon his collar.

"I come to you, Rev. Thorne, upon a matter of life
and death because I am familiar with your work in the
London police from the newspaper reports of the
scandalous Brownloe case," he had begun in a
querulous voice. "And yet I fear that there are some
details which I must insist upon withholding even
from you. I am, however, assured that I can tell you
everything that you will need to know in order to
conduct your investigation and perhaps to save an
innocent man from the gallows. May I continue with
my story on those terms, Rev. Thorne?"

My friend had chuckled quietly and then replied:

"Father, my curate Knowles will, I am sure, attest that I normally tolerate no conditions when I undertake anything; however, I must admit to being somewhat intrigued. Your case promises some points of novelty. Pray continue, sir, though I venture that you never imagined yourself engaging the services of even a retired detective when you were a student at Oxford under the stern eye of the Rev. Cuthbert Eager."

"Indeed not, Rev. Thorne," had responded our guest without commenting on Thorne's observation. "But time is of the essence. Pray let me first tell you of the strange circumstances under which I came to meet the young man who stands in danger of wrongful arrest for murder."

"Do so," my friend Thorne had encouraged, and then with a glance in my direction had added, "This case, Knowles, may well provide the opportunity for you to display again those skills of acute observation which you put to such good use in the unfortunate matter of the murder of Miss Susan Phillips last September. Proceed, Father."

Thus it was that in the early evening of an April afternoon in 1912, I took up my pen to make notes on the extraordinary narrative of the anonymous clerical gentleman:

"Firstly, you must know," our visitor began, "that I value my privacy. Only the most urgent need has brought me to consult you and that not without considerable hesitation and reservation. I shall tell you nothing of myself, not my name, not even the location of the parish in which I reside, nor will I tell you how I came to meet the young man whose very life I place in your hands or where he is currently in hiding. These details are, let me again assure you Rev. Thorne, quite irrelevant to the case, which I will now outline.

"I ask you to imagine a young man recently released from His Majesty's Prison after serving ten years at hard labor for a robbery with violence committed (for he was, indeed, guilty, and he richly deserved the punishment which the judge handed down) when he was an impulsive youth of fifteen. Let us suppose the young man to be a reformed character determined never to see the inside of a jail again. What hope does such a man have of employment? None, Rev. Thorne, none! So, the young man changes his name and invents a past for himself in Australia – all supported by documents and references. They are forgeries, of course, but the young man still has some connections in the criminal underworld, and he has no scruple about using them towards the end of securing legal employment.

"Let us further imagine that this young man eventually (it is not easy) gains employment in a position of trust in a small firm which sells antique jewelry and that for two years all goes well. He works diligently, has a natural aptitude for the business, and wins the trust of his employer. Then, one dreadful morning, he arrives at his place of business, finds the door to the premises open, and upon entering sees the body of his employer lying prone by the open safe. He naturally rushes to offer assistance but realizes almost immediately that his employer is dead. Imagine, at that very moment, that a police constable enters the shop, sees the opened safe and the body with our young man stooped over it, and jumps to the obvious conclusion. The young man is startled by the constable's shouts and he panics: he does the one thing that confirms his guilt – he brushes the constable aside and runs. Such is the story that I was told by the young man himself yesterday evening, Rev. Thorne."

"By Jove," I exclaimed, "the Reginald Scott case!"

"Quite so, Knowles," Thorne replied. "Kindly read the account of the case in today's Times of London."

I crossed the room and extracted from a pile of newspapers on Thorne's writing desk The Times of London for Wednesday, April 24th 1912.

"Horrible Murder of Jewelry Merchant," I began. "At about 7.40 on Tuesday morning, a police constable, being alerted to a disturbance at the premises of Mr. Winfred Styles in Bond Street, entered the property to find a robbery in progress. Despite his best efforts, the constable was unable to apprehend the robber and found, on his return to the premises, the dead body of Mr. Styles in front of an empty safe. The robber appears to have got away with the entire contents of the safe thought to include a number of valuable items of antique jewelry as well as a sum of over £1,000 in cash.

"Medical reports indicate that Mr. Styles had been attacked from the rear and struck with a heavy object resulting in almost immediate death. Scotland Yard police are seeking to apprehend Mr. Reginald Scott who has been employed at the premises for about two years. Mr. Scott did not report for work today, and a description provided by Mr. Styles' assistant John Thorson matches that of the man seen running from the premises which was given by the constable. Inspector Cousins of Scotland Yard expressed himself confident of an early arrest."

"Now let me see," Rev. Thorne said reflectively, "I believe that the Stop Press column reported that the hunt for Mr. Scott still continues. He proves elusive. I wonder where he can be. Well, since you, sir, have made it clear that you will confirm no personal details, let us continue to imagine.

"Say that Mr. Reginald Scott makes good his escape from the immediate vicinity of the crime, and only then realizes the fatal error he has made – had he stayed, the fact that the contents of the safe were not in his possession would surely have indicated his innocence. Now, however, he has had the opportunity to hide what was stolen, so he cannot return, for if he does then his entire deception will be revealed – Reginald Scott, late of Australia, being a complete fabrication. This will confirm his guilt in the minds of the official police who, not noted for their imagination, will dismiss out of hand his account of arriving to find his employer already dead, and so he will be tried, convicted and executed, though the stolen property will never be recovered. Not, on the whole, an attractive proposition for the young man.

"So he flees. Perhaps he goes only a few miles or perhaps he journeys further, but let us imagine that somewhere in the South East of England (your accent, sir, excludes all else) he encounters a clergyman - perhaps in a church or a church yard. The desperate young man recognizes a fellow Catholic, begs the clergyman to take his confession, and afterwards throws himself on the priest's mercy. This clergyman is by nature trusting. Besides, he can reveal nothing that he has been told without breaking the confidentiality of the confessional. The young man is successfully hidden from view, and the clergyman (unable for obvious reasons to consult the official police) seeks the assistance of an unofficial detective who has, nevertheless, a certain degree of credibility because of his years in the force. How do we do in our imaginings, sir?"

"Very plausible, Rev. Thorne, as a purely hypothetical outline," conceded our client. "And now I beg you to investigate this case. If the man who calls himself Reginald Scott is not the murderer and thief, then you have only to find the real culprit to prove his innocence. I urge you to visit the scene of the crime tomorrow morning. Good day gentlemen."

At that moment, our mysterious visitor unexpectedly rose and made as though to leave, prompting Rev. Thorne to exclaim:

"But, sir, if I do accept your, shall we say 'challenge', how am I to contact you?"

"You will not contact me, Rev. Thorne," came the stern reply, "nor will you take any steps to ascertain my identity. You will find the true murderer of Mr. Styles and, if possible, recover the stolen property. I shall follow reports of the case in the newspapers and, assuming that you exonerate the young man, I shall call upon you again. Upon that you have my word."

With those words, the cleric strode vigorously towards the door and was gone. I looked towards Thorne in some amazement, but he was already half way across the room, and in a few more seconds he threw me my overcoat saying:

"Follow him, Knowles! Do not return until you know his identity. Be careful. He will be on the alert."

With that, Thorne all but bundled me out of the door, and having allowed a few seconds to pass in the hall I emerged into the gathering darkness of Waterloo Crescent. Immediately I caught sight of our client already fifty yards away walking rapidly northwards towards the railway station, and I proceeded, with the greatest caution, to follow him. Once or twice, indeed, he did look back as though checking that he was not being observed, but I was able to anticipate his actions and evaded detection. He entered a small commercial hotel adjacent to the station, and ten minutes later I followed and made discreet enquiries at the reception desk.

"The clerical gentleman?" the clerk responded to my question. "Oh, that gentleman is not a guest at the hotel. He left by the rear exit just after he arrived. He did, however, leave this note addressed to a Mr. Knowles if that is your name, sir."

I took the note, opened it, and read, "Knowles, For God's sake convince Rev. Thorne to take this case. The life of an innocent young man hangs by a thread." There was not a signature, but then I had not expected one.

You may guess that I returned to Waterloo Crescent somewhat chastened by my failure, but to my surprise and relief Thorne appeared surprisingly sanguine about my failure and commenting only that, since we could not locate Reginald Scott through our client, then we should have to do so in the manner suggested by our client.

Thursday morning found Rev. Thorne and myself at Sanditon Station in time to catch the 6.30 a.m. train which, with one connection, delivered us to Victoria Station in London by 9.00 a.m. A hansom cab took us to Scotland Yard where Inspector Cousins, alerted by a telegraph Thorne had sent the previous evening, was waiting to accompany us to the premises of Mr. Winfred Styles in Bond Street. The Inspector had expressed great surprise at Rev. Thorne's interest in the case, but he had been advised by his colleagues to humor Thorne's whims and so had readily agreed to accompany us to the scene of the murder. The business, as you can imagine, was closed, but we were admitted by Mr. Styles' assistant John Thorson, a single man in his mid-thirties who lived in rooms on the third floor of the building.

Thorne conducted a meticulous inspection of the safe and the surrounding areas which served only to confirm what was already known: the safe had been opened by someone who knew the combination and everything of value had been taken from it. All that remained were some legal papers of no value to anyone other than Mr. Styles. There was no sign of forced entry to the premises. Rev. Thorne turned to Thorson.

"On Tuesday morning, Mr. Thorson, you heard nothing?" he asked.

"No, sir," Thorson stated. "My rooms are right on the top floor, and my bedroom is in the rear of the building. I was shaving when I was alerted by the constable's whistle, so I got dressed quickly and ran down the stairs to find the constable leaning over the body of Mr. Styles. The constable informed me that

Mr. Styles was dead, that the safe had been robbed, and that he had chased a man out of the shop. He described the man, and I recognized Mr. Scott immediately."

"Was it usual for Mr. Styles to be on the premises at such an early hour?" Thorne continued.

"Indeed, not, sir. Most unusual," Thorson replied. "Normally, Mr. Scott arrives at about 7.30 a.m., and he unlocks the front door. I come down at 8 a.m., and together we prepare to open at 9.00 a.m., by which time Mr. Styles is normally here."

"And did either Scott or yourself have the combination to the safe?" asked Thorne.

"Neither one, sir," answered Thorson. "Mr. Styles was the only person who had that information, though there is a copy deposited at the bank for use in an emergency."

"Have you any idea why Mr. Styles should have broken his routine yesterday – why he should have wanted to open the safe so early?" Thorne inquired.

"No particular knowledge, sir. No," Thorson replied. "But, though it was unusual, it was not entirely unheard of. Very occasionally, Mr. Styles would come to the premises before opening hours to take something from the safe."

"How often did that happen?" Thorne continued.

"Seldom, sir. Perhaps five times each year. For example, if Mr. Styles wished to take a particularly valuable piece to show to a client who was not able to come to his place of business," Thorson stated.

Rev. Thorne thanked and dismissed Thorson, and turning to Cousins asked to speak with the constable who had discovered the robbery in progress.

Constable O'Brien referred to his notebook as he gave the following account:

"I was on my normal beat on Tuesday morning, sir, and I entered Bond Street at about 7.30 a.m. The street was deserted, as it usually is at that hour. There were just a few lights beginning to come on in the rooms above the business premises. I had begun checking the doors of the shops to ensure that they were locked when I felt a small stone hit me on the shoulder. I immediately assumed that it was some street urchin playing a prank, but by the time I turned the street was again deserted. Knowing that there is only one hiding place in the area from which the stone must have been thrown, a small alley at the side of Mr. Styles' shop, I ran towards it, but just before I reached the alley I noticed that the door to Mr. Style's business was slightly ajar. Looking in, I saw a man, who I now know to have been Mr. Reginald Scott, bent over the safe. I did not at that time actually see the body of Mr. Styles since it was lying on the floor and was therefore obscured from my view. When I shouted, the man turned and ran. I tried to stop him, but he pushed me aside. I rushed outside, blew my whistle three times, and attempted a pursuit; however, I soon realized that I had no chance of overtaking the man who was clearly quite young and fit, so I returned here to discover the victim who I found to be dead. Mr. Thorson came running down the stairs (he still had shaving soap on his face), and on my describing the man who I had seen, he said that the description matched that of Mr. Reginald Scott."

"And did you search the alleyway, constable?" Thorne asked.

"No, sir, I did not. I had something more important to do than to chase childish practical jokers," the constable replied rather disdainfully.

"Constable O'Brien," pronounced Rev. Thorne solemnly, "I fear that you will never rise in your chosen profession."

Five minutes later, Thorne and I were in the narrow alley which ran between the premises belonging to Mr. Styles and the next shop. Even in the mid-morning sun, the alley was a dark and obscure place, and the heavy bars on the ground floor windows of the premises on each side lent it a sinister air. Whilst Thorne examined every surface with his lens, I worked my way to the rear of the buildings where I found that a wall at least twenty-feet high had been built, effectively blocking any exit from the alley. The red brick wall itself offered neither foot nor handholds, nor was there anything at all in the alley which might have been used to scale it. This raised, of course, the obvious question of where the urchin who had thrown the pebble at the constable had gone. When I returned to Thorne, I described what I had found and added the only explanation which I could think of.

"I suppose that the child waited in the darkness of the alley until the constable went into the shop and then made his escape," I suggested.

"Perhaps, Knowles," mused Thorne. "But why would a street urchin, who we must presume to be familiar with the local area, have run into a blind alley? Had Constable O'Brien not been distracted by the robbery in progress, the child would have been trapped."

Thorne paused gazing up at the sliver of blue sky visible between the tops of the two buildings. Then he continued, "I wonder, Knowles, if you recall Mr. Poe's account of the famous investigation of Monsieur Dupin in 1841 concerning the murders in the Rue Morgue?"

"Good Lord, Rev. Thorne," I burst out exasperated. "You surely do not mean to suggest that we are looking for an orangutan!"

"Hardly," Thorne replied laughing loudly, "but as I recall, the essential clue which enabled Dupin to solve that mystery had to do with climbing the unclimbable."

"But Thorne," I objected forcefully. "There is no way that a human could possibly climb the wall at the rear of the alley or either of the buildings on each side - or an orangutan either for that matter."

"I do not suggest that the child climbed the wall, Knowles. I merely suggest that, once a person has entered this alley, the only way out of it must be to climb," Thorne said definitively.

My friend stood beneath a second floor window on Mr. Styles' side of the alley and looked upward. Unlike those on the ground floor, neither the second or third floor windows had bars. Suddenly, Thorne knelt down and began to search in a small clump of weeds which struggled towards the light. With an exclamation of satisfaction, he rose holding in his fingers a delicate earring which he dropped into my outstretched palm.

"Good Lord, Thorne!" I exclaimed. "How did you ever find that?"

"I found it, Knowles," Thorne replied, "because I was looking for it. If I am not mistaken, our case is nearly complete. I think that we merely need to examine the other side of that second floor window where, unless I miss my guess, we shall find some indications of a rope having been secured and let down into the alley."

As we walked through the shop, Thorne assured Inspector Cousins that he would have something to report within a few minutes and urged him to remain. Cousins agreed, though with some evident impatience. Together, Thorne and I climbed the stairs to the second floor which had originally been a living and storage area for the business below but was now largely unused. The room which we entered had once been a bedroom, though it had clearly not been used for some years. Thorne began to examine the window. It was obvious to me from the accumulation of dust and cobwebs that this window had seldom been opened in the past, but there were clear signs that it had been opened at least once fairly recently. Thorne then took his lens, a small pair of tweezers and an envelope from his coat pocket and began picking tiny threads from the window ledge and the floorboards. On his hands and knees, he moved from the window to one of the feet of the cast iron bedstead.

"Notice, Knowles," Thorne instructed, "how the rope has been tied around this leg of the bed. There are signs of abrasion in a narrow band here. You see that some of the paint has flaked off from the iron. I also draw your attention to the movement of the bedstead caused by the weight of a man climbing up the rope."

Although the flakes of paint were evident, I did not, in point of fact, see the evidence of movement to which Thorne had alluded, but not wanting to appear foolish I let this pass, for Thorne frequently saw things which were invisible to me. Having completed his examination, he rose slowly, sealed the envelope containing the fibers and handed it to me. Without saying anything, he turned and led the way to the shop where Cousins was waiting with signs of growing frustration.

"Well, Thorne," he began, "you do not appear to have found Mr. Scott. Does the official police force have your permission to continue its search for the murderer?"

Rev. Thorne ignored the sarcasm evident in Cousins' tone.

"A case not without its points of interest, Inspector," Thorne began. "I draw your attention to this earring which I found in the alleyway under the second floor window of the room where I have just recovered these strands of fiber. I am sure that analysis will show them to be hemp. They come from a rope which was secured around the foot of an old bedstead, the other end being thrown out of the window. If you search Mr. Thorson's rooms, I have no doubt that you will find the other earring. I believe that you will also find Mr. Styles' appointment book, and that the entry for Tuesday, 23rd April, will read that he had an appointment later in the day with a very wealthy, and perhaps a very elderly, client. That is how the thief knew that Mr. Styles would open the safe on Tuesday morning before the business opened. As for the rope, doubtless it is still on the premises somewhere. I fancy that you will find it knotted at fairly regular intervals to facilitate climbing. Put together, that should be sufficient evident for you to arrest Mr. Thorson. Good day, Cousins."

Thorne and I returned to Sanditon and were taking tea together in Waterloo Crescent when, at approximately 4.00 p.m., we received the following note from Cousins by special delivery:

"Correct in every detail Rev. Thorne! Please forgive my rudeness this morning. I really should have given more credit to your reputation amongst those colleagues of mine who worked with you. Styles' appointment book was found stuffed at the back of a drawer in Thorson's dressing room. The earring was more difficult to locate, but eventually we found it under Thorson's bed where it had doubtless rolled when he was going through the contents of the safe. A hempen rope was discovered in one of the outhouses – knots and all.

"I take my hat off to you, Thorne. This time it appears that you have saved an innocent man from the gallows. I have, of course, as you requested, publically called off the search for Mr. Reginald Scott since he is no longer a suspect.

"Sincerely, Cousins."

Thorne had penned a brief reply and given it to the messenger boy. News of the arrest of Mr. John Thorson on the charge of robbery and murder made the final edition of Thursday's London Evening Standard which we, of course, received only on

Friday morning. Reading his copy over breakfast, Thorne predicted confidently that we should receive a visit from our anonymous client later that day. Thus it was no surprise when, about an hour after we had completed breakfast, Elizabeth entered and announced, "The nice clerical gentleman is waiting to see Rev. Thorne, if you please sirs."

Seated in the same deep armchair from which he had told his remarkable story, our client smiled benevolently and offered his congratulations.

"Really, Rev. Thorne," he began, "you have exceeded even my own expectations. I can assure you that Mr. Scott is tremendously relieved, and I am sure that in a day or so, when he has recovered from the stress of recent events, he will be here in person to express his gratitude. In lieu of which, I very much hope that you will accept this sum. Oh, I know that you will not accept any personal payment, sir, but I am quite sure that there are charitable works in the parish for which it might be used. I am not a rich man, Rev. Thorne, but I am not poor either, and the services which you have performed for my young friend must not be undervalued."

Our client rose and placed an envelope in Thorne's hand. My friend received it from him, and then, to my astonishment, he grasped a handful of our cleric's hair and pulled violently. To my further astonishment, the hair came away in his hand revealing the short-cropped, dark hair of a young man beneath.

"Allow me, Knowles," began Thorne, "to introduce you to Mr. Reginald Scott, our client."

Scott had almost instantly recovered his composure and began laughing heartily.

"Rev. Thorne, I really have underestimated you!" he cried. "You had no connection at all with my original arrest and conviction, though I heard your name often enough in jail – and not spoken of too kindly I can assure you. How long have you known, sir?"

"You will recall, Mr. Scott that I made reference to your being a theology student at Oxford under the stern eye of the Rev. Cuthbert Eager," Rev. Thorne explained. "It may interest you to know that that learned gentleman has been dead for a hundred years. I must compliment you, however, on a most effective way of evading the searching eyes of the official police force."

At that moment, Elizabeth appeared again and, to my astonishment, ushered Inspector Cousins into the room.

"Ah, Cousins! What a happy coincidence," cried Thorne. "I was just talking to my friend Mr. Reginald Scott about the tenacity of the British police."

As though on cue, Cousins stepped forward and with a practiced hand placed handcuffs on our client saying, "Mr. Reginald Scott, I arrest you for the murder of Mr. Styles and for robbery." Turning to Thorne he continued, "Rev. Thorne, you will be glad to know that John Thorson was released from custody at 9.00 a.m. this morning as you requested in your note. He was mightily relieved I can tell you. I might add, sir," Cousins concluded ironically, "that if you ever begin to find the life of a vicar in Sanditon a little too quiet, the Metropolitan Police is always on the look-out for likely recruits. I should be happy to put in a good word for you. Good day gentlemen."

All of this happened so rapidly that our client had not opportunity to speak. Indeed, he was removed by Cousins before he could do more than begin loudly to protest his innocence, which he did all of the way down the hallway and into the street. From the front window of our sitting room, Thorne and I observed our clerical client being hustled into a Black Maria.

"A most inventive mind, Knowles," said Thorne with something like admiration in his tone. "Reginald Scott intended to prove his own innocence and to have an innocent man convicted; he planned to do it on the unimpeachable evidence of retired Detective Sergeant Lyle Thorne. And he almost pulled it off!"

"But how, Thorne, did you know? When did you know?" I stammered.

"Oh come, Knowles," Thorne began, "the art of the illusionist is to convince his audience that they have seen something which they have not, in fact, seen. We see the saw, held by the stage magician, appear to go through the lady's body, we hear her cry out, and we assume that we must have seen her cut in half. We believe this even though we know perfectly well that the same young lady was cut in half yesterday and will be cut in half tomorrow on the very same stage without suffering any adverse consequences. Of course, there never was a street urchin: that was a pure invention of the constable's. He imagined what he expected to see, and Cousins believed the illusion of the urchin because the constable himself believed it. The master illusionist Scott wanted us two to imagine John Thorson attacking Mr. Styles, removing the valuables from the safe and then waiting in the alley for Scott to arrive and enter the shop at his normal time. We were to believe that we had seen Thorson attracting the attention of the constable by throwing a small stone, running into the alley, and making his escape with the contents of the safe by using a rope which he then pulled up after him, just at the moment when the innocent Reginald Scott was being discovered at the scene of the robbery and murder. That is what the illusionist meant us to see, and I must admit that for a moment that is what I saw.

"The earring was suggestive, of course, but not conclusive. Thorson could conceivably have dropped it as he made his escape, but it was just a little too convenient for it to be found there. What finally convinced me that the person who attracted the constable's attention by throwing a pebble did not run into the alley but rather ran into the already open door of the shop (which is not three feet before the alley) was the movement of the cast iron bedstead to which I drew your attention."

"But Thorne," I protested, "I could see no evidence that the bedstead had moved at all."

"That, my dear friend, is what I drew to your attention. Clearly a rope had been hung out of the window, but not on the morning of the robbery, and no one had ever climbed that rope or the bedstead would have been pulled across the floor. And did it not occur to you that there were rather too many hemp fibers? The earring (a rather inferior piece which would hardly need the security of a safe) could have been planted days before. If you recall, I mentioned that I only found it because I was looking for it, and I was looking for it because I was

41

beginning to suspect that the lady had not been cut in half at all. After that, I believe I followed the path which Scott laid down for me rather well."

"Then, you knew that Thorson was innocent, Thorne!" I exclaimed allowing my feeling of resentment full rein. "Why did you not tell me?"

"Because, Knowles, the illusion had to be played out to the end. Had Scott not been totally convinced that he had been exonerated, he would never have returned to Waterloo Crescent, and you surely do not think that our colleagues in the uniformed branch would ever have found him. A murderer would have escaped justice."

I saw the logic of Rev. Thorne's reasoning, but still I felt that I had been manipulated by him as a pawn in a game which he had thoroughly enjoyed playing.

The Case of the Italian Bride
May 1913

I would rather share one lifetime with you
than face all the ages of this world alone.
(J.R.R. Tolkien, *The Fellowship of the Ring*)

If ex-Detective Sergeant Lyle Thorne had anticipated a quiet, uneventful life as the Vicar of Sanditon when he took up the post in 1907, then the four years during which I served as his curate must have been a grave disappointment to him. The publicity which attended the dramatic trial at Lewes Assizes of Mrs. Brownloe for the murder of Miss Phillips inevitably highlighted my friend's role in bringing to light the truth of Miss Phillips' supposed fall, and the Old Bailey trial and conviction of Reginald Scott for robbery and murder brought Thorne even greater notoriety.

Thus, I was not entirely surprised one early summer afternoon to observe Inspector Campbell opening the gate and walking down the path to the vicarage. Campbell had developed the habit of calling on Thorne at irregular intervals whenever he wished to discuss a particular investigation, but he had not visited for about three months, and I noted that he had put on a little weight around the waist.

When Elizabeth showed our visitor into the sitting room, Thorne requested that she prepare a tea for three.

"Elizabeth," Campbell interjected, "would you be so kind as to make that four?"

"Certainly, sir," our housekeeper replied. "I shall have it ready in half an hour."

When Elizabeth had retired, Inspector Campbell offered an explanation:

"I hope that you will not mind Rev. Thorne, but I have taken the liberty of suggesting to a young man with whom I spoke this morning that he should he call here at 4 p.m. He has a story which might intrigue you. It's nothing that the official police could act upon, of course, but it might be just your kind of thing."

Perhaps reacting more to the glint in Campbell's eye that to the professional's rather dismissive tone, Thorne replied, "I should be only too delighted to hear something a little original. To be honest with you, Campbell, my young curate leaves me very little to do in the parish." Then he added inconsequentially, "Besides, I am pleased to see, my friend, that you have abandoned the reprehensible habit of smoking. Or, at least, that you have stopped smoking cigarettes, since you clearly keep to your occasional pipe. That cannot have been easy at a time when you are so dissatisfied with your new maid."

"Come now, Thorne!" Campbell cried. "This is some trick played upon me by my wife! I told her at lunchtime that I was planning to visit you, and she has telephoned you with these details."

Whilst I knew this to be untrue, I was at a loss to see how Thorne had reached his conclusions.

"Quite unnecessary, Campbell," my friend replied. "In your days as a smoker of cigarettes, you were always negligent of the ash. It invariably fell onto the lapels of your Norfolk jackets. No amount of brushing would entirely clean them. Yet now I observe spotless lapels and that, combined with a significant reduction of the nicotine staining of the index finger of your right hand, points to only one conclusion. On the other hand, the blackening of the skin at the end of that same index finger (the finger which you use to compress the tobacco in your pipe) tells me you have not yet abandoned that particular vice."

"Well then," Campbell remarked, obviously somewhat disappointed by the simplicity of the deductions, "that was not so remarkable after all, but how do you know of our troubles with Mary?"

"That your new maid is called Mary, I did not know, but that you have a new maid is clear from the state of your coat and jacket. The coat which you carry on your arm is missing one button on the sleeve, and another hangs by a thread. Whilst I have remarked on the cleanliness of the front of your jacket (brushed, I assume, by yourself), the same may not be said of the back which shows signs of having been brushed, if at all, most negligently. This is not the work of the excellent Jenny; therefore, I assume that a new, and altogether inferior, young woman has been employed."

Campbell laughed quietly, and then admitted, "But Thorne, it is all true. Mary is a constant disappointment, though she came to us with a glowing testimonial."

"One might almost suspect, Knowles," Thorne added, glancing across at me mischievously, "that her previous employers were particularly anxious to dispense with her services."

At that moment Elizabeth returned with a tray containing an excellent high tea for four.

"Begging your pardon, Rev. Thorne," Elizabeth began, "but there is a young man at the door who seems very anxious to speak with you. I told him that you had a visitor and that it might not be convenient, but he implored that I should ask."

"Campbell you have become my good angel," said Rev. Thorne. "You have not been here for thirty minutes and already comes an anxious young man - an event which seems highly promising. Elizabeth, please show in this anxious young man. Whatever it is that brings him here, he will undoubtedly benefit from a cup of your good, strong tea and some of these excellent scones."

When our visitor was shown in, Campbell introduced him to us as Mr. Arthur Rolands. He appeared to me to be no more than twenty years of age, somewhat of my own height though of a slimmer build. He was smartly, but not expensively, dressed in a manner that immediately suggested to me a bank clerk. I noted a narrow gold wedding ring on the third finger of his left hand and wondered that one so young, with such obviously limited financial means, should be married.

"Pray be seated Mr. Arthur Rolands and do have some of Elizabeth's sandwiches and her finest scones and fruit cake with your tea. You must forgive the scrutiny of my curate, Mr. Knowles, who has already noted your youth, your, may I say, modest circumstances, and the wedding band on your finger, and is as puzzled by this combination of circumstances as am I. I am even more anxious to know what has impelled you to take a leave of absence from your place of employment (a bank, I fancy) in Lewes and travel by railway to consult me on so very warm a Friday afternoon."

The young man found a sudden difficulty in digesting the sandwich he was eating, and Campbell laughed aloud now that he was in the position to watch the impact of Thorne's deductions on someone else.

"How do you know where I am employed, Rev. Thorne?" Rolands asked.

"I observed from your jacket and from the front of your shirt," began Rev. Thorne, "that you had taken a train this afternoon. Your compartment was full, otherwise you would surely not have chosen to sit facing the engine, and the other people in the compartment, no doubt feeling the heat of the day, insisted on having the window open which accounts for the soot smuts on your jacket and shirt, Mr. Rolands."

Taking a clean handkerchief from his breast pocket and wiping it first across the top and then along the sole of Arthur Roland's right shoe, Thorne continued, "All that remains is to determine your point of departure. The town of Lewes is built upon Wealden clay, but clays are very individual. No two are the same. The Wealden clay has a distinctive yellow hue that is quite unique." At this point Rev. Thorne held up the evidence of the residue on the handkerchief and then concluded, "As for your profession, every item of your dress suggests a clerk in a bank, including (and especially) the shine and wear on you right jacket sleeve which results from much writing."

"Accurate in every detail, sir!" our guest declared in delight. "It seems that Inspector Campbell was correct in suggesting that you might see to the bottom of a puzzle that has me completely baffled and seems to have thoroughly upset my wife."

Rev. Thorne was suddenly transformed. Gone was his lightness and humor, and in their place only concentration and concern. He filled his tea cup, settled deeply into his armchair, and then looked our visitor squarely in the eye.

"Pray tell me everything relating to the matter" he said. "Leave out nothing, however trivial. Knowles, you may wish to take a few notes of the salient points. And now, Mr. Roland, proceed."

Our visitor took a final sip of tea and began his remarkable narrative:

"My name is Arthur Roland, and I am twenty-one years of age. I have worked for the Colonial and Empire Merchant Bank for five years and am currently in the position of junior clerk at the Lewes branch, as you surmised. My salary is not great, but I have been assured that the Bank thinks highly of my work and that I have a secure future with them. Were that not so, I could never have contemplated marriage at so young an age. Six months ago, I married Maria Bentonni, a young lady of only eighteen years. Since that also must strike anyone as strange, I will explain the circumstances.

"Miss Bentonni came to England as a child of seven with her father, a widower from Southern Italy. Mr. Bentonni was a wealthy businessman who had occasion regularly to visit the London branch of the Colonial and Empire Bank. Before his death a year ago, he was for some time rather ill, and Maria, by then a young woman, accompanied him on his visits. That was my first acquaintance with her, though, of course, at that time our relationship was both distant and purely professional. However, I may admit to you, Rev. Thorne, that even then I could not be entirely indifferent to Maria's beauty."

Our visitor paused and seemed a little embarrassed by his frank admission.

"Maria and I were thrown together much more following Mr. Bentonni's death. As I told you, he was a wealthy man, and disposing of his assets in accordance with his will was a complex matter. Since I had been administering his accounts, it fell to me (of course, under the direction of a senior at the Bank) to administer many of the financial details consequent upon his will. In this way, I discovered that Maria was left only with a small allowance until such time as she should return to her home in Italy which was an explicit stipulation in the will. Maria, however, made it perfectly clear to me that she had no wish to return to Italy. You will understand that she had grown up in England and regarded it as her home. I also flatter myself that her feelings for me were part of the equation that made her determined to stay in England, for by this time our professional relationship had developed into friendship. Perhaps I should say, sir, that it had developed into something more than friendship.

"It was specified in a telegram from the Italian family immediately following her father's death that Maria should lodge, temporarily, with some distant relations in Wembley. These people closely supervised Maria so that she had very little freedom. This made it difficult for us to meet, but we nevertheless contrived to do so without the knowledge or permission of her relatives, who would certainly have objected to our doing so. Unhappy as she was with these arrangements, and unhappy as I was that I could see so very little of her, we agreed that we should marry immediately. The Bank was good enough to grant my request for a transfer to the Lewes branch, both Maria and I being anxious to remove ourselves from the influence of the relations in Wembley. My own parents, although not rich, took pity on us and gave us enough money to set up house together in Sanditon. Effectively, we eloped only informing Maria's Italian family after the marriage hoping thereby to gain their acceptance of the union as a fait accompli.

"What can I say? Our first months of marriage were as perfect as I could have imagined them. On my income, we managed to hire a daily maid, and whilst I went to work Maria set about transforming our house into a beautiful home. Maria's only unhappiness came whenever she received letters from her family in Italy. These came regularly each week, and though she made every effort to hide her emotions I knew that she would sit weeping silently for hours after reading them.

"The first sign of anything unusual, I now realize, was the disappearance of my fountain pen. It seemed so entirely trivial at the time, if rather aggravating. One Monday morning, as I was preparing to leave for the bank, I could not find my fountain pen. I knew that I had had it the day before since I had used it to write some letters, but I simply could not locate it. Well, I assumed that it had rolled under a piece of furniture, so when I left for work that day I asked Maria to search the house. When I returned that evening, Maria told me that she had been quite unable to find the pen, but had purchased another for me. I was so delighted with this gift from my wife (the new pen being somewhat superior to the one I had lost) that I thought no more about it.

"Our life proceeded as before, with Maria more loving and more beautiful each day, if that were possible. The only slight cloud on our happiness was the weekly letters. Then, three weeks after the disappearance of the pen, a silver salt seller also disappeared. The thing in itself was not of particular value, but it had been part of a set which my parents had given to us as a wedding gift, and so it had more than normal value. It seemed to me that the only explanation could be that our maid had stolen both of the missing items. When I told Maria of my suspicions, she defended the maid most strongly and begged me not to accuse her. However, when I asked my wife for any alternative explanation, she was unable to suggest one. I dismissed the maid despite her passionate protestations of innocence and Maria's tearful pleading that she be given another chance. We found a new maid with no difficulty. However, after what happened last night, I fear that I may have committed a grave injustice in dismissing that girl."

Arthur Roland paused as though to gather his thoughts to explain the final element of his story.

"And what, pray, happened last night?" prompted Rev. Thorne.

"My wife and I retired at 10 p.m. as normal. I watched Maria take off her wedding ring and place it in a small box on the table beside the bed as she does every night. Rev. Thorne, when we awoke this morning, the ring had vanished! The box was still on the table, but the ring was no longer in it."

"And precisely how was the loss discovered?" asked Rev. Thorne.

"My wife awoke before me as is usual, and, as she always does, her first action was to put the ring on her finger. When she saw that it was not there, she screamed, and that woke me. She was terribly upset, and I was forced to apply smelling salts for I feared that she would faint. I wanted to stay to look after her, but shortly Maria recovered her composure. She insisted on my going to work as usual, and assured me that when the maid arrived she would be well looked after and that together they would find the ring. Reluctantly I did as she wished, but before taking my usual train to Lewes I called in at the Sanditon police station and talked to Inspector Cousins. He said he was sure that my wife had already found the ring, but he did suggest that I might meet him here should I continue to be concerned. My mind has not been easy all day, sir, so I left work early to come to see you. What does it mean Rev. Thorne? What does it mean?"

"Tell me more precisely," Thorne began, "about your wife's reaction to the first two thefts."

"She seemed to regard the loss of the pen as a rather amusing mystery, but when she discovered the loss of the silver salt pot, I noticed that her face went deadly pale, and I that for several days she seemed distracted as though lost in her own thoughts."

"Describe the windows in your house, if you would," Thorne requested.

"They are single sash-cord windows, Rev. Thorne. During the day when it is warm they are normally left open to air the house, but when I get home one of my tasks is to ensure that each one is locked before we retire to bed," Roland explained, and an uneasy silence fell on the room which was interrupted by Inspector Cousins.

"So you see, Thorne," he began, "that when this gentleman came to me with his story this morning, I really could not help him. What! Send a policeman round to find a pen, a salt pot and a ring that Mrs. Roland had misplaced somewhere – I should have been laughed out of the service. Nevertheless, there was something about his story which just did not sit right with me, so, I advised Mr. Roland to go to work as usual, and if he was still concerned to meet me here. Now, Thorne, did I do the right thing, or are we both wasting your time?"

Thorne wafted away the question with a movement of his right hand as though he had been wafting away a troublesome fly. Then he pressed together the fingers of his hands and sat motionless for ten minutes, after which time he sprang from his chair to consult one of the many reference books which littered his desk. Having apparently found the information for which he was searching, Thorne turned again to our visitors.

"Cousins," he began in a serious tone, "you have done well in bringing this case to my attention. I cannot say that everything is clear to me yet, but I do not doubt that we must move quickly if we are to save Mrs. Roland. I pray that we are not already too late!"

Arthur Roland's face eloquently expressed his growing dismay, but Thorne was quick to reassure him, "I almost certainly overstate the danger, Mr. Roland. These people seem to prefer to work during the hours of darkness. I have no doubt that we shall thwart them if you will do exactly as I say. Do not deviate from my instructions in the slightest matter – your future happiness may depend upon it.

"Take a cab home with Knowles. Knowles, you must be sure to wear your hat and to take one of the walking sticks from the hall – a heavy one. When you arrive home, Mr. Roland, dismiss the maid and make your wife secure in a safe place – a cellar, a loft, anywhere in the house except where she might be expected to be. Then you must take Knowles's coat and hat and leave. You may take a cab to Waterloo Crescent where you will await our return."

"Rev. Thorne, I certainly will not leave my wife if, as you claim, she is in any danger!" cried our visitor.

"It is essential that you should leave so that it appears to anyone observing the house that you have called a clergyman to minister to your wife in her distress and that, the clergyman having left, you and your wife are at home as normal. If your wife is in danger (and it is possible that she is in mortal danger), you could not place her in better hands than those of Knowles. There is not another man in England to whom you may with more assurance entrust the protection of your wife."

"Thorne your confidence in me is flattering, but what must I do when Mr. Roland leaves?" I asked.

"First Knowles, make sure that Mrs. Roland is safe - that above everything! Close and lock all of the windows being sure that you are not seen, then go to the bedroom. At 10 p.m., being sure to cast no shadows on the curtain, lock that window and extinguish the light. Then, wait with your walking stick at the ready. I have no time to explain further, but strike at any intruder. Do not hesitate. Strike hard, for the man will be armed with a knife."

Arthur Roland gave a stifled gasp.

"Do not be too alarmed Mr. Roland," Thorne added, "perhaps nothing at all will happen tonight, but we cannot be too careful. Now go, for there is not a moment to lose. Cousins, would you be so good as to have two constables in the general area of Mr. Roland's residence tonight? Tell them to keep out of sight but to be ready for any disturbance."

Rev. Thorne's manner suggested the utmost urgency, so I found neither the opportunity nor the need to ask him what he planned to do. I knew enough to trust implicitly to his judgment. Roland and I left the vicarage and hailed a cab in the Crescent.

Our journey through the gathering gloom of the evening seemed endless, the very traffic conspiring to delay us on every street. My companion was in a paroxysm of anxiety about his wife. I really think that Rev. Thorne's warning was the first time that Roland had considered that his wife's safety, even her life, might be in danger. However, when we arrived at the house, we were both relieved to discover that nothing out of the ordinary had happened during the day, and that the maid had left at her usual time of 6.00 p.m. Mrs. Roland appeared outwardly calm and now seemed disposed to regard the disappearance of the ring as a minor and temporary inconvenience despite the fact that she and the maid had searched the house from top to bottom without success. As I looked more closely into Mrs. Roland's young and beautiful Italian face, however, the nervous tension was clear to see.

When I outlined Rev. Thorne's plan, Mrs. Roland vigorously denied that she was in any danger, yet from her agitation I judged her to be in great fear. I proceeded exactly as Thorne had directed. Arthur Roland put my overcoat on over his, took a walking stick of his own from a stand in the hall, and with the collar turned up and the hat tilted over his face walked briskly to the cab which I had asked to wait in front of the house and left for Waterloo Crescent. I prevailed upon Mrs. Roland to sleep in the attic room, secured the downstairs windows, and took up my station in the main bedroom.

Being careful not to show myself, I pulled down the sash window and slotted the bolt across. Then, I drew the curtains together and settled into the armchair to wait. At 10 p.m., I turned out the gaslight as Thorne had instructed and resumed my vigil. The weight of the walking stick, which I grasped firmly in my right hand, pressed hard upon my thigh.

In the darkness, I completely lost track of time. It may have been an hour later or it may have been five, when I was alerted by the faintest sound of something scraping against the outside windowsill and then of metal grating upon metal – unmistakably the sound of the window lock being opened gently from the outside with the aid of a long-bladed knife. Suddenly alert, I waited until I saw the window itself being slid almost imperceptibly upwards and the curtains eased back to reveal a man's silhouette black against the grey night sky.

I rushed at the figure with the stick upraised and brought it down on the man's back breaking the window pane in so doing. The man gasped in pain, so I knew that I had made firm contact, but the figure turned and disappeared from the window into the darkness below with a speed that quite astounded me. Almost immediately, I heard a sharp cry of pain. In the blackness of the garden, a desperate struggle seemed to be taking place, but I could make out nothing of the combatants except vague, indistinct outlines. Next, I heard a solid blow struck followed by a deep grown. The following silence was abruptly broken by the sound of Rev. Thorne's voice:

"It's all right Knowles! I have him. I believe that Mrs. Roland will be quite safe now. Be so good as to find a policeman. I fancy that Cousins has men close by," he shouted up at the window.

The following morning Rev. Thorne and I sat in the vicarage dining room sharing a breakfast with Inspector Cousins, our young client and his younger wife.

"But what I still do not understand, Thorne, is how you knew that Mrs. Roland was in danger," stated the Inspector.

"Mrs. Roland," began Thorne addressing our beautiful guest in the most reassuring of tones, "you will please correct me if I am in error. However, I fear that, much as you undoubtedly love your husband, there were aspects of your life about which you chose to tell him nothing."

"You are right, Rev. Thorne, and I now see how much harm that nearly caused." At this point, she reached out for her husband's hand and with hardly suppressed emotion cried, "I must ask your forgiveness, Arthur. I did not realize the danger in which I was placing us both. It is time to tell everything."

Thorne took this as his cue, "The Bentonni family is indeed from Southern Italy, more specifically from Sicily. The family (forgive me, Mrs. Roland) has for generations been associated with crime, but the Omertà, the particular code of silence to which natives of the island adhere, has made it impossible for the authorities to bring them to justice. Nevertheless, some years ago, the head of the Bentonni family found it expedient to come to England where he had, over the years, invested much of the family's considerable wealth in legitimate businesses. When her father died, I suspect that Maria Bentonni saw the opportunity to begin a new life, particularly since she had fallen in love with a man who knew nothing of her family connections."

Mrs. Roland gave the slightest nod in the direction of Thorne to indicate the accuracy of his account thus far.

"I suspect that the Bentonni family would have done everything possible to prevent the marriage, but events overtook them. Nevertheless, they were not to be underestimated, and their determined aim became to return the lady to the land of her birth and to the 'protection' of her family. When appeals failed (those weekly letters which so affected your wife, Mr. Roland), an agent of the family was dispatched to bring her back, by force if necessary, though they still hoped to persuade her to return home, albeit by the use of threats. The thefts were a clear message that the family could reach her at any time, and I am sure, madam, that you understood them as such, at least after the silver salt seller disappeared."

Again Mrs. Roland made the slightest nod and concluded the story herself:

"At first the letters from my family pleaded with me in the most loving terms to return to Sicily, but, when I proved obstinate, their tone became threatening. After the second theft, I knew, Rev. Thorne. You see, they took a wedding gift to make it clear that they expected me to go with them," Mrs. Roland explained. "When they took my wedding ring, I was in despair for I knew that they had the power to carry me away by force whenever they chose and that they would have no compunctions about doing so, but I still could not bring myself to tell my dear Arthur the truth which I had hidden from him for so long. I now know that my lack of honesty could have cost us both our lives. I am so sorry."

The Colonial and Empire Bank did indeed value the services of Mr. Arthur Roland, so much so that, at the urgent request of my friend, who had in his time with the Metropolitan Police been of some service to that institution, the bank transferred him to its Dublin branch, where, at the urging of Rev. Thorne, the couple began a new life together under a different family name.

Only my duty to present to the public the facts of this remarkable case compels me to conclude this account with a newspaper cutting from The Irish Times dated 3rd July, 1914:

"HUSBAND AND WIFE KILLED
IN DROWNING TRAGEDY

"The bodies of Mr. Ronald Bennett (23) and his young wife were recovered yesterday from the waters off Howth Point. It appears that the two were walking beside the cliffs when they were overtaken by the swiftness of the in-coming tide and pulled out to sea by the strong current.

"The police report states that the bodies were found washed ashore on rocks south of the Point. Both bodies had suffered extensive injuries as a result of the action of the waves in dashing them onto the rocks at the foot of the cliff.

"An unexplained feature of the accident is that Mr. and Mrs. Bennett's wedding rings were each missing and have not yet been recovered.

"Mr. Bennett was a highly respected clerk with the Colonial and Empire Bank in Queenstown. His wife is thought to have spent her childhood in Southern Italy. There were no children.

"An inquest will be held…"

The Case of the Missing Betrothed
August 1913

> Life can only be understood backwards; but it
> must be lived forwards.
> (Søren Kierkegaard, *Journals and Papers*)

In the many years of my friendship with Rev. Lyle
Thorne, I had ample evidence of the strength of his
constitution. I served as his curate from 1910 to 1914,
and during that period, one of the few illnesses which
ever confined Thorne to his bed for any length of time
occurred during the late summer of 1913. Despite
suffering from a slight cough, Rev. Thorne had
unwisely attended a Thursday evening performance at
the Sanditon Lyceum and had been caught in a
sudden, drenching downpour upon his return home.
Within hours, he had begun to exhibit the clearest
signs of fever, and an anxious Elizabeth had
telephoned for the doctor who had immediately
diagnosed influenza. For the next five days, during
which I was at his side almost continuously, I had
been quite anxious about his condition. However, on
the morning of the fifth day his fever broke, and he
was able to sit up in bed and take a little breakfast.
The doctor called at 9.30 a.m. and expressed himself
convinced that, although he would be very weak for
several more days, Thorne was out of danger and on
the road to recovery.

The doctor had suggested that Thorne should
spend the day in the lounge downstairs, and I had just
left him sleeping peacefully on the chaise longue,

taking care to leave the dining room door slightly ajar so that I could hear if he awoke, when Elizabeth knocked quietly on the door and entered.

"Excuse me, Mr. Knowles, sir, but there is a young gentleman. He wished to speak with Rev. Thorne. I told him that Rev. Thorne is seriously ill and can't be disturbed, but he says he must talk with him. He seems terribly distressed, sir. It would be an act of charity if you would see him yourself."

"Show the gentleman in if you will Elizabeth," I said, "but tell him to speak softly. Rev. Thorne is sleeping."

Moments later, Elizabeth ushered into the room a man in his early twenties who was dressed in a morning suit of superior cut though his collar was open at the neck and he wore no tie. I would have called the gentleman handsome had not his unshaven chin and the dark circles under his eyes given his face a haggard and prematurely aged look. My visitor hesitantly walked towards me and extended his hand.

"Mr. Knowles?" he asked in a voice scarcely above a whisper. "Thank you for seeing me. My name is Dominic Rufford. I had hoped to enlist the assistance of Rev. Thorne in solving a mystery which threatens my entire happiness, but, since he is not well, I throw myself on your mercy. I am aware, sir, from newspaper reports of your association with Rev. Thorne, and I know that you have assisted him on some of his most celebrated cases. Please help me now. I am at my wits' end and have neither slept nor eaten for two days."

"Mr. Rufford, please sit down and compose yourself," I replied. "Rev. Thorne is far too ill to undertake any kind of investigation. I would certainly help you if I could, but you seem to over-estimate the contribution which I have made to my friend's investigations. I have no skill in detection, as Rev. Thorne is constantly reminding me; my role has merely been to observe and to assist at his direction. I fear that your journey from Boxcomb Place has been wasted: I am not the man to solve the mystery of the disappearance of your betrothed."

It was only the look of surprise and the sudden paleness of Dominic Rufford's face that made me aware of the full significance of what I had just said.

"Mr. Knowles," he stammered, "how could you possibly know? The affair has been kept out of the papers."

"My dear sir, it is simplicity itself," I explained. "You yourself told me your name. Had I nothing more to go on than the name, and the quality and impeccable cut of your suit, I should have at least thought of the Ruffords of Boxcomb Place – one of the oldest and richest families in Sussex."

At this point, I moved to the corner of the room where I had been piling the daily papers against Thorne's recovery and found a copy of The London Times for June 28th, 1913.

"However, since I read a few days ago," I continued, "this brief announcement in The Times, 'Mr. Thomas Simmons announces that his only daughter, Merissa Simmons, will marry Mr. Dominic Rufford in Boxcomb Place Church on Saturday, August 1st, speculation was quite unnecessary. As to the cause of your visit, that was simplicity itself. Clearly you are distraught, and over what may a bridegroom be distraught except the loss of his bride? Consider also that today is Monday, August 3rd and that you told me that you had neither eaten nor slept for two days, that is, since the day of your planned marriage.

"Now, had the young lady been taken ill, you would certainly have contacted a doctor; had she suddenly eloped (forgive me, Mr. Rufford, it happens more often than you might imagine) with another man, you would presumably have contacted a lawyer. However, since you chose to consult The Rev. Lyle Thorne, and not in his capacity as Vicar of Sanditon but because of his reputation as an investigator, the only possible explanation is that your bride-to-be has quite literally disappeared (you referred to your case as a "mystery"), and that the local police have proved unable to help."

"Correct in every detail, sir!" my visitor asserted, not neglecting in his excitement to keep his voice at the level of an excited whisper. "Please, allow me to set out the facts of the case before you decide."

"Very well, Mr. Rufford," I replied, still more than a little surprised by what I had just heard myself say, "but I promise nothing."

"I understand, sir. It will be a relief simply to tell someone what has happened."

And so began the most remarkable narrative of Mr. Dominic Rufford:

"As you mentioned, Mr. Knowles, my family has owned lands in Sussex for centuries. Boxcomb Place Hall was built in the mid-Seventeenth Century, and the family has occupied it uninterrupted from the Restoration of Charles II to the present day. Sadly, I never met my father; he died in a tragic hunting accident when I was a few months old. Mother never re-married, and as a result I was her only child. When my dear mother passed away some five years ago, my inheritance was held in trust until my twenty-first birthday. However, I effectively became the master of Boxcomb Place Hall at the age of nineteen, though being a student at that time I was in residence there only during the Oxford vacations.

"It was less than a month after my mother's death that Mr. Thomas Simmons, a widower, purchased an extensive property known as The Manor in the nearby village of Fernham. Mr. Simmons is an intensely private man who has come to be disliked in the village because from the first he seemed determined to take no part in its social life, something which the villagers had come to expect from whoever occupied The Manor. To me, however, he has always been kindness itself.

"We met quite by chance and in the least propitious of circumstances. In the days and weeks following the death of my mother, I had developed the habit of taking long solitary walks in the summer evenings. I always followed the same route which took me through the grounds of The Manor, a trespass which I justified because I knew that the property had been without a tenant for two years or more. Well, one evening, as I approached the entrance to the main drive, I saw the figure of a man with an open shotgun leaning one foot on the five-barred gate which was, for the first time in my memory, closed and padlocked.

At first, I really thought that he was going to shoot me for the man raised his shotgun and warned me to be off in the most unfriendly of terms. I was both shocked and, quite frankly, rather scared, but something in my reaction must have convinced the man that I meant no ill, and when he saw this, his manner towards me changed completely, and we fell to talking. When he learned my identity, Mr. Simmons' entire demeanor softened; he informed me that he had heard of my recent loss from the local newspaper, and I think he took pity on me. Howsoever, I became a regular visitor at The Manor whenever I was in residence at the Hall, and it is there that I met his daughter, Miss Merissa Simmons, who was then a mere child of fifteen.

"Over the next few years, my acquaintance with Mr. Simmons developed into a profound friendship. Indeed, I truly believe that I was the only friend he had in the world, for there were never any other visitors at The Manor. The house itself is kept by only one servant, a distinguished-looking man of Far Eastern origin who Mr. Simmons only ever called Le Clerke. Perhaps Mr. Simmons saw in me the son he had never had; I certainly came to regard him as the father I had never known. We shared an interesting in fishing, riding and shooting - the normal country pursuits.

For most of the year, Merissa, Miss Simmons, was away at a private school, in Switzerland I believe, but when she returned for the holidays, Mr. Simmons encouraged me to visit The Manor as often as I could. He kept himself resolutely aloof from the life of the village, and I think he felt that his daughter would be lonely, though, in fact, Merissa so adored her father that she never showed the slightest unhappiness with the quiet life which she lived whilst at The Manor.

"Well, Merissa's school days ended, and she came to live permanently at The Manor. Within a year, I came down from Oxford and took up residence full-time at Boxcomb Place Hall where I set about a program of rebuilding and refurbishment which was long overdue. Now eighteen, Merissa had become a beautiful young woman, and I realized that our former intimacy was no longer appropriate, particularly as I began to sense that my own feelings toward the young lady were changing from those of innocent friendship to love. Thus, whenever I came to The Manor (and Mr. Simmons continued to invited me frequently), I made sure to spend the time always in her father's company and seldom, as we had used to do so often, to be alone with Merissa.

"I saw from Merissa's face that this change in our relationship was troubling to her, but I could find no way to explain it without having to acknowledge my feelings which I was too fainthearted to do.

"Things came to a head on Christmas Day two years ago. I had spent the day pleasantly enough at The Manor, but as I was leaving, Merissa followed me to the stables and so contrived to speak with me alone.

"'Dominic, why are you avoiding me?' she cried in a voice betraying hardly suppressed emotion, 'Have I done something to offend you?'

"I assured her that there was not offence, but she immediately described my changed behavior, giving details of each perceived slight in such detail that I knew that I would not be able to escape without offering some explanation.

"'It is only this,' I told her. 'I think that you have hardly noticed that you are now a young woman. You will make your own choice… You will… I mean, your father will wish you… to marry.' I was painfully aware of my own inability to put into words what it was that I wished to say, but Merissa surprised me by breaking into a delighted laugh.

"'And this is all?' she asked, and then went on without giving me the opportunity to answer. 'And who would my father have me marry if not one of the richest men in Sussex, particularly since I should marry him if he were one of the poorest? Dominic, if you have anything like the same feelings for me that I have for you, I think it rather urgent that you talk to my father about the matter and get his blessing.'"

Dominic Rufford was silent and seemed lost in thought. I prompted him by asking about Mr. Simon's reaction to his revelation.

"It was entirely unexpected, Mr. Knowles" he continued, "and I was very glad that I had sought a private interview with him so that Merissa did not have to witness it. At the first mention of my feelings for his daughter, I saw by the look on his face that the idea that we two might become lovers had quite simply never occurred to him. It seemed that he had come to regard us as brother and sister, and he remained frozen in speechless shock for several seconds. Then I witnessed once again that dangerous anger which had so terrified me at our first meeting, and when he spoke, it was in the same harsh and threatening tone.

"'How dare you!' he raged. 'To come into my house… to abuse my kindness…'

"And then, just as suddenly as his anger had erupted, it evaporated entirely, and Thomas Simmons was once again my mentor and friend.

"'Well, well,' he began, haltingly 'forgive my rudeness, my dear boy. I was just a little taken aback at first, but it was perhaps only to be expected that you two… and who could ask for a more distinguished son-in-law?... I couldn't hope to keep Merissa to myself, you know," he said with a chuckle as though I had just suggested so absurd a thing, and then he continued in the most affable manner, "Of course, you have my consent and my blessing, but my daughter is not yet nineteen. We must wait at least until you have completed the work on Boxcomb Place Hall. Yes, two years. And then, if your feelings and my daughter's are as they are now, as I am sure that they will be, you may marry. Quietly, you know. I will have not great ado for, as you have good reason to understand, I am not drawn to social ostentation."

"Thus it was that, the two years having passed, Merissa and I became engaged in January. When it came to our wedding, Mr. Simmons insisted on a private affair to which Merissa and I were only too happy to agree. The only exception was the short notice which I myself inserted in The Times without consulting Mr. Simmons, and which I am convinced that he did not see for no London newspapers are delivered to the Manor."

My visitor had lapsed again into thoughtful silence, so I once again prompted him to explain the details of Merissa Simmons' disappearance.

"Every arrangement for the wedding seemed to go smoothly. We were to honeymoon in Italy, and last Friday afternoon I sent over my automobile and Merissa was driven into Lewes to pick up a bonnet which she had ordered and to do some final shopping. The automobile stopped outside the milliner's shop in the high street, and my driver, Travis, saw her enter the shop. Mr. Knowles, she has not been seen since! The alarm was raised by my driver when Merissa did not meet him at the appointed place and time. Once I had driven over and informed him, Mr. Simmons and I rushed to Lewes, the police were alerted, but it was already getting late and our exhaustive search revealed nothing. It was as though Merissa had vanished into thin air."

"Of the many possible explanations, I believe that is the least likely," I commented, "but tell me, how did Mr. Simmons react to the news of his daughter's disappearance?"

"Most strangely, Mr. Knowles," Dominic Rufford answered. "He was, of course, shocked, and his first words were largely incoherent and addressed more to himself than to me. 'Fool that I am!' he exclaimed, 'This is my own doing. Oh that I had refused you both, but how could I refuse her anything?' I could make nothing of this, but as so often with Thomas Simmons he collected himself almost at once and took charge of things.

"As I told you, we drove into Lewes immediately in my automobile, and when our initial search revealed nothing it was Mr. Simmons who informed the police. By then, of course, it was getting quite late and nothing much could be done that night. At his suggestion, Mr. Simmons spent Friday, Saturday and Sunday nights at the Hall with me, and each day we renewed the search. However, when on Sunday evening the local police reported that they had no clues whatsoever, I decided on my own initiative to consult Rev. Thorne."

"You have done well to do so, Mr. Dominic Rufford," the voice of Rev. Thorne came weakly from the lounge and drew us both to my friend's side. "Though you would have done better to have come at once, but there is still a hope that the trail is not entirely cold. You must return home immediately and insist that Mr. Simmons spends the evening at Boxcomb Place Hall – it is quite possible that he is himself in some danger. As you see, I am myself too weak to travel to Lewes, but my curate will take the 11.45 a.m. train and will undoubtedly call upon you this evening. You may have complete confidence in him. Good day, sir."

Once I had ushered our puzzled client to the door, I returned to Thorne and began to protest that there could be no point in my visiting Lewes. Thorne, however, abruptly cut me off.

"Knowles," he said sharply, "a young woman's happiness and – just possibly – her life are at stake, and if you do not go then at least one will most certainly be lost. Spend the afternoon in Lewes. Someone must have seen something; as you said yourself, young women do not simply vanish into thin air in English market towns! You know my methods better than any man in England, apply them. In the evening, go to Boxcomb Place Hall and insist that Rufford and Simmons accompany you to the Manor.

Plan to arrive there at 10 p.m., for by then the solution to this mystery should be clear. No questions, Knowles," Rev. Thorne's instructions were interrupted by a spasm of violent coughing, "I am really too exhausted to contribute any more to this investigation."

So saying, Rev. Thorne allowed his head to fall back onto the cushion, closed his eyes wearily, and I left him sleeping deeply. Thorne's instructions seemed to me to be both precise and utterly meaningless, yet I knew better than to question his judgment, so I quickly packed an overnight bag and made my way to Sanditon Station.

I alighted onto the platform of Lewes Station at 12.30 p.m., and, having deposited my bag at the left luggage office, I walked from there to the High Street. There was only one milliner's shop, so I went in. When the assistants understood that I was seeking information on Miss Simmons' disappearance, they were most anxious to help; clearly the local antipathy which Rufford had reported towards the father did not extend to the daughter. A few questions confirmed everything that Dominic Rufford had told me: Miss Simmons had entered the shop at about 2.00 p.m., had purchased a bonnet and two pairs of leather gloves, and had left the shop at about 2.30 p.m. She had talked excitedly about her coming wedding, spoken with anticipation of seeing Florence, Naples, Rome, and had appeared to be in the most excellent spirits. The young woman who had served her had noticed Miss Simmons turn left out of the shop to walk down the High Street, which is to say in the direction which she would have needed to take in order to meet Rufford's driver Travis.

Extensive enquiries at shops all along the High Street failed to produce any further information. A carter, who had not been questioned by the police, recalled having glimpsed a young woman of Miss Simmons' age at about the right time deep in earnest conversation with a gentleman of Oriental appearance. However, he did not think it in the least suspicious and was not even able to say for certain that the woman he had seen was Miss Simmons. I felt that I was simply repeating the same fruitless enquiries as the official police, and I wondered how Thorne would have approached the investigation.

By this time, the afternoon was almost over, and I realized that I had had nothing to eat that day since breakfast. I had noticed a tea room directly opposite the milliner's, so I returned to it and selected a table by the window which gave me the very clearest view of the door to the milliner's. As I waited for the tea which I had ordered, I occupied my time between thinking through the riddle of the young lady's disappearance and glancing at that shop doorway as though by doing so I might make the lady suddenly reappear.

There were, it seemed to me, only three possibilities: Miss Simmons had arranged the whole thing to avoid her marriage, which seemed unlikely if I believed Dominic Rufford's account, and I did; she had been forcibly abducted, which I immediately discounted because it would surely have attracted some attention, which it did not; or she had gone willingly with her abductor(s) either because she knew them or because they immediately won her trust. Stated in this way, I felt sure that Miss Simmons had gone willingly, but I still did not know why or with whom.

Someone had waited for Miss Simmons to emerge from the milliner's shop (perhaps the carter's Oriental gentleman, perhaps not), and had then persuaded her to go with him. They had probably disappeared in seconds down one of the side streets where he had an automobile or a carriage waiting. I was again gazing at the milliner's doorway when it suddenly struck me that I might be sitting at the very same table which the abductor had used whilst waiting for Miss Simmons to leave the milliner's. She had been driven to the door by Travis, Dominic Rufford's man, so there would have been no opportunity to abduct her then. If someone wished to intercept her as she came out of the milliner's then he or she could hardly loiter in the street. There was no place less conspicuous in which to wait than the busy tea room. – hiding in plain sight so to speak.

As the waitress placed a tray on my table and began to set tea before me, I determined to test my theory.

"Excellent, err…," I began, and then paused as though trying to recollect her name.

"Joanne, sir," the waitress prompted.

"Joanne to be sure," I said in a tone suggesting humorous delight. "I shall forget my own name next. And my friend said that I must come in here and have your high tea, and that I must ask for Joanne. He was in here only last Friday, just after two in the afternoon

– sat at a table by the window. Do you recall him? An Oriental gentleman?"

"Oh yes sir," the waitress began eagerly, "I remember the gentleman you mean. Indeed, he sat right here, looking out of the window, just as you have been doing. He was very polite, very complimentary about the tea, but he had to leave most abruptly with half of it unfinished. I wondered for a moment if he had run out without paying, but when I examined the table he had left a whole guinea!"

I left the tea rooms refreshed and suddenly quite hopeful. I had at least gathered two pieces of evidence which the local police appeared to have missed, and I felt sure that Thorne would be able to make something of them even if I could not.

Having retrieved my overnight bag from the station, I went immediately to The Bell where I took a room for the night and hired a cab to take me to Boxcomb Place. I arrived at 9.00 p.m. Dominic Rufford was delighted to see me; Thomas Simmons significantly less so. Rufford pressed me for an account of my enquiries, but I was evasive, hinting only that I had made some progress in identifying Miss Simmon's abductor. I said that it was essential to the investigation that we all go immediately to The Manor.

"Really, Mr. Knowles," Simmons objected angrily, "I cannot see any conceivable point in going there. To tell you the truth, I am less than happy with my dear friend Dominic for involving Rev. Thorne and yourself in this matter at all. To my way of thinking, this is a family matter which the official police should investigate not some amateur investigator."

In truth, I could not myself see what it was that Thorne had in mind in having us all go to The Manor, but I knew better than to question my friend's judgment, so I blustered.

"I can assure you both," I stated with a confidence I certainly did not feel, "that the solution to the mystery lies at The Manor. Come, it is time for us to depart."

I dismissed the driver of the gig which I had hired. The three of us traveled in Rufford's automobile, and a solemn trio we made for scarcely a word was spoken on the entire journey. Darkness had finally fallen as Travis turned from the roadway through the five-barred gate which marked the beginning of the driveway to The Manor. As we approached the steps to the front door, Mr. Simmons suddenly sprang from the auto, walked quickly up to the door, and beat upon it with his stick.

"Le Clerke! Open up. We have visitors!" he called several times.

The door had not been opened by the time that Rufford and I joined Simmons on the threshold. Simmons turned towards us.

"It is as I feared, gentlemen, a wasted trip" he began. "Le Clerke has clearly gone to bed for the night. We shall not wake him now; his hearing is very poor these days. Perhaps we might return tomorrow morning."

At the very moment when Simmons turned away from the door and attempted to usher us down the steps towards the automobile, the front door opened slowly, and there stood Rev. Lyle Thorne.

"Forgive me for keeping you waiting gentlemen," he said. "Monsieur Le Clerke is temporarily unavailable, and I fear that I am not quite so well acquainted with the house as I should like to be. Do please come in. Mr. Simmons, should you be contemplating an escape, may I draw your attention to the constable standing beside the gate? Let me assure you that he is not alone."

With an angry scowl, Simmons swept past Thorne and, entering the sitting room, threw himself down upon a sofa.

"Allow me to introduce," began Thorne directing Rufford and myself into the sitting room, "Mr. Simon Thompson, sometime manager of the Bank of Singapore. I would also introduce you to Mr. Bineesh Ong, sometime chief cashier at the same bank, but he is currently (as the euphemism goes) helping the police with their inquiries."

"Damn you, Thorne!" shouted the old man from the couch. "How did you know?"

"When the manager of the Bank of Singapore disappeared almost fifteen years ago, Scotland Yard, of course, was consulted. The Bank offered to pay all expenses if a detective could be sent, and I was approached. At first, the case interested me a good deal, so much so that I was almost tempted to visit the Far East. It appeared that the manager, Mr. Simon Thompson, had walked out of the bank at the end of the day's business and simply disappeared. Equally mysteriously, Mr. Thomson's five-year-old daughter had likewise disappeared from her school in the middle of the day. Blood-soaked garments belonging to Thompson and to his daughter were found, and for a while suspicion fell on Mr. Bineesh Ong, the bank's chief cashier, who had also vanished.

"It seemed, at first, to be a mystery worthy of my modest skills. However, when it became clear that a considerable sum of money was also unaccounted for, I concluded that here was a case of petty theft, albeit one which involved over five hundred thousand pounds, and I rapidly lost interest. Another officer was dispatched to Singapore, and I understand that he had some success in tracing the movements of the three fugitives, but that the trail went cold in San Paulo, Brazil."

"And what," asked the defeated man on the couch, "convinced you that I was guilty and not the victim of a kidnapping or murder?"

"The disappearance of your daughter, sir," replied Thorne. "Your wife had died giving birth to a second child, a baby boy who lived for only six months, and by all accounts, from that moment on, you became totally devoted to your daughter. Had you been abducted or murdered, there was no reason at all for the perpetrator to take your child, whereas if you had gone of your own free will, you would certainly not have left without her. And now, Mr. Thompson, if you would kindly step outside this room, I believe that you will find a police inspector who is most anxious that you should accompany him to Lewes police station and answer some further questions."

Mr. Simon Thompson rose from the couch with a groan. He turned to Rufford and said:

"I really am sorry, my boy, but Mr. Ong would not allow the marriage to go forward. The publicity, you see, would have ruined everything. I had bought myself two years' grace, but you were both still determined to go through with it. I tried to restrain Mr. Ong, but he acted on his own initiative."

Thompson left the room without a backward glance. Dominic Rufford's face became a mask of grief and his head sank into his hands.

"My God, Thorne!" I exclaimed when the man had left the room. "Do you mean to tell us that Miss Simmons is dead?"

"Calmly, my dear Knowles. You will agitate our young friend Rufford. I think that we all need a cup of tea to calm our frayed nerves. Be so kind as to ring for it."

Extremely puzzled by Thorne's command, I crossed the room and gave two sharp tugs on the bell. Almost immediately, a young woman appeared carrying a tray.

"Dominic," she said softly, and in a moment, the tray having crashed to the floor, Dominic Rufford held the young woman in his arms.

"Oh dear!" Thorne exclaimed, "I fear, Knowles, that my weakness for the dramatic has robbed us of our tea and cost Mr. Simmons a fine set of china. However, he will probably have no further use for it. Moreover, I think we may still be in time for supper at The Bell. I have a police automobile waiting. Mr. Rufford, you would perhaps like to take Miss Simmons to Boxcomb Place Hall, I am sure that there is a great deal that you wish to say to each other. We will call upon you at 10 a.m. tomorrow morning, if that is convenient. Good evening."

Dominic Rufford, still holding Miss Simmons in his arms, said only, "Thank you, Rev. Thorne. Thank you, Mr. Knowles."

On the following morning, Rev. Thorne and I found ourselves in the library at Boxcomb Place Hall. I had already explained the reasoning which had led me to conclude that Miss Simmons had been approached shortly after leaving the milliner's by an Asian gentleman who, it was now clear, was the man Dominic Rufford had known as Le Clerke.

"Miss Simmons was not alarmed when she was approached because, of course, Le Clerke was familiar to her. I assume, Miss, that he told you some story which quickly won your confidence?" I ventured.

"That is true, Mr. Knowles," she replied. "He told me that my father had been taken ill, and that I had to return to The Manor immediately. He had the automobile waiting in one of the side streets, and he drove me to the door. Once I entered, my father admitted that the story of his being taken ill was untrue. He told me, however, an even more frightening story. He said that news of the wedding had alerted an enemy of his from the past to his whereabouts, and that we must leave the country immediately or his life would be in the gravest danger. I had long sensed that my father's secluded life in the Sussex countryside was a result of something that had happened when he was in the Far East, though none of my efforts to get his to talk about it ever had any success. Of course, I begged to speak with Dominic, but he insisted that not only was his life in danger but mine also. He assured me that the separation would be only temporary, but that until we could leave the area I must have no contact with anyone.

"The sounds fantastic enough now, Rev. Thorne, but you must recall that it was my father telling me this. I had never in my life had occasion to doubt him or to question his love for me, so I agreed to remain indoors under the careful watch of Le Clerke. I only realized that his story was a tissue of lies when you came to The Manor yesterday with the police and Le Clerke was arrested."

"But how did you know that Miss Simmons was at The Manor, Thorne?" I asked.

"Because, my dear Knowles, it was the one place where no one had looked for her. You will recall that in his original narrative Mr. Rufford told us that Mr. Simmons, having spent Friday evening searching Lewes insisted on staying the night with him at Boscomb Place Hall rather than returning to The Manor and that he did the same on Saturday and Sunday evenings. That struck me as significant. It was to ensure that Rufford should not approach The Manor. Simmons was taking no chance that his daughter should see or be seen by the man she loved."

"What will happen to my father now, Rev. Thorne?" asked the young woman.

"I fear that he and his accomplice will spend the rest of their lives in jail. If it is any consolation, I am sure that his love for you was genuine. He may have persuaded himself that he acted out of fear of being detected, but I think that the true motive was his fear of losing you."

Two hours later, Rev. Thorne and I were sitting in a first class non-smoking compartment on our way back to Sanditon.

"I fear, Knowles," Thorne began, "that on Monday morning I was not quite so sick as I led you to believe. Forgive me. It was essential for Mr. Simon Thompson to believe that I was not actively involved in the case or he might have taken some more desperate action before it was in our power to prevent it."

"So my own investigations were pointless," I stated with more than a hint of bitterness in my voice.

"Not at all, Knowles. If you will recall, you reached exactly the same conclusions as did I without having the prior knowledge which I had. Had I not been able to get to The Manor, the door would have been opened by Mr. Bineesh Ong, and you would quickly have closed the case," Thorne replied.

This appeared to be a rather charitable view of my own endeavors, but I accepted it gratefully.

"And how is your health now, my friend?" I asked concerned that the exertions of the last twenty-four hours might have had a debilitating effect.

"Capital, my dear fellow," replied Thorne. "I believe that I never felt better in my life!"

The Case of the Hanging Man
August 1927

> Men in general judge more from appearances than
> from reality. All men have eyes, but few have the
> gift of penetration.
> (Nicolo Machiavelli, *The Prince*)

Arthur Mee's guide to the county of Sussex briefly
describes the village of Upper Sanditon thus:

"Six miles inland from the resort town of
Sanditon, at the head of the valley where the Dover
Brook tumbles down from the escarpment of the
Weald on its short journey to the sea, lies the
picturesque village of Upper Sanditon. The village
has been by-passed by the major roads and by the
railway, and thus it retains the character of former
centuries. Upper Sanditon is much the more ancient
of the two settlements having been founded in Saxon
times, and it boasts one of the finest unrestored
Norman churches in the South of England. Visitors
may see in the nave the magnificent tomb of Roger of
Bordeaux, who fought with William the Conqueror at
Hastings. The bell tower is reputed to be the tallest in
Sussex."

It was here that, in the spring of 1927, The Rev.
Lyle Thorne purchased a small farmhouse to which
he retired - for a second time.

I had not seen my old mentor and friend for
several years, most of which I had spent as a minister
in India. The visit was prompted by a telegram from
Thorne following the tragic death of my wife in

Bombay three months previously. Thus, having returned to England in July and having settled some legal affairs, one glorious morning in late summer I took the train from Victoria Station to Sanditon. Pausing in Sanditon only to take a walk around Waterloo Crescent and to survey the vicarage from a distance, I hired a cab to take me the five or six miles to Thorne's new home.

My first sight of Rev. Thorne was enough to reassure me that the quiet life of the Southern Downs agreed with his constitution. Eight months earlier, when he had announced in a letter his intention finally to retire and to vacate the vicarage at Sanditon which had been the center of his intellectual universe for two decades, I had been seriously concerned that, without the constant stimulation provided by his spiritual vocation, and by the occasional problems which were brought to him, Rev. Thorne might, in his mid-sixties, fall into a slow decline. Now, however, as I walked down the long pathway to the farmhouse, I saw that he was positively thriving on the change of environment. His frame, still slim, had filled out a little (I estimated that his weight had increased by at least twenty pounds), and his face, angular and intense as always, had lost some of that gaunt look which the strain of his two professions had deeply etched upon it over the years.

Before my arrival, Rev. Thorne had evidently been busily engaged in some procedure in the large glasshouse at the far end of his garden, for upon hearing the automobile which had brought me from

Sanditon he strode towards me with a trowel in his left hand.

"Knowles," said he vigorously shaking my hand, "I trust that you had a pleasant journey. Take a seat here in the garden, and I shall wash my hands and bring out some tea. It is all prepared for your arrival, although I doubt that you will find it up to the standard of our Elizabeth."

Then, almost as an after-thought, Rev. Thorne added, "I am sincerely sorry for your loss, Knowles."

He paused and his shoulders slumped somewhat before, by an effort of will, he recovered his upright posture and continued, "Hopefully, a few weeks of peace and quiet in the Sussex countryside, watching the leaves turn from green to gold, will have a soothing and healthful effect."

No more was said on this painful subject by my friend; what had been said (and more what had been communicated without words) was enough.

During the rest of the afternoon and evening, Thorne described the gentle rhythm into which his life had fallen since moving into the farmhouse, his plans to renovate the house, and the progress which he was making in growing exotic orchids. When I ventured to hint at my fear that, after a working lifetime spent first in London and then in Sanditon, he might find himself bored by the quiet of the countryside, Rev. Thorne laughed.

"I believe, my dear Knowles, that someone once remarked that the English village has more potential for crime than does the English city. You would scarcely believe the machinations and deceptions of Upper Sanditon. I am myself only beginning to appreciate the subtle nuances of its society – its petty feuds and jealousies, its ancient quarrels, and its secret love affairs. Then again, when my fellow humans fail to provide me with sufficient puzzles, I have always my orchids to fall back on," he concluded.

In this pleasant way, the first few hours of my stay with Thorne came to an end, and, upon retiring to the bedroom which Thorne had prepared for my use, I fell immediately (and for the first time in several months) into a deep and restful sleep the moment my head touched the pillow.

I was woken early the next morning by the jangling and disharmonious sound of church bells being rung most inexpertly. I saw from my pocket watch that it was still only 6.30 a.m. and wondered that anyone should wish the bells to peal (and so discordantly) at such an hour. Further sleep being quite out of the question, I completed my toilet and made my way downstairs. In the parlor, I found Thorne, not normally an early-riser, already sitting down to a breakfast of eggs and bacon.

"Knowles," he began, "please be so good as to pour yourself some tea, and I will begin cooking your breakfast. I thought that you would be tired after your travels and did not expect you to come down for an hour or two yet."

"I should not have," I complained irritably, "had it not been for the confounded bells of your local church. I suppose that bell-ringers do have to practice, but is it really their custom to do it at so early an hour?"

Thorne was about to reply when we both heard the unmistakable sound of a trotting horse in the lane, and a few moments later that of someone running down the path towards the farmhouse. A fist pounded urgently five times upon the door. Thorne exchanged a quizzical glance with me and sprang to open the door revealing a rather portly, middle-aged village constable who was breathing heavily and clearly in a considerable state of agitation.

"Rev. Thorne," the man began breathlessly, "please come with me, sir. I need your help as I am over my head in this affair. I can explain everything as we ride along, but you must come immediately, if you would be so kind."

"Knowles," said Rev. Thorne calmly, "allow me to introduce Constable Poole. Poole, this is my friend and former curate Mr. Knowles. There is room in the carriage for three I take it?"

Constable Poole readily assented to my accompanying himself and Rev. Thorne, and as he drove to the village he told his remarkable narrative:

"It began this morning with the ringing of the bells. I am sure that you heard them. Everyone in the village did, and quite a crowd had gathered outside the church by the time I got there not five minutes after the bells had fallen silent. The church door was open, which is unusual because a few years ago some vagrants got into the church at night and stole a valuable cross, and since then the vicar always keeps the door locked. When I entered the church, I found that the door to the bell tower was locked from the inside. Neither the vicar nor the curate was present, and I was pretty much stumped, until I noticed that

Harry Bailey, the village blacksmith, was amongst the crowd and that he was carrying his hammer, so I ordered him to break the door down. Fortunately, Harry was more level-headed than was I, and he proceeded to remove the hinges. It did not take Harry much more than five minutes to get the door off, and then we could see into the ground floor of the tower…"

Here the constable paused and added parenthetically, "Terrible sight, Rev. Thorne, and I hope never again to see anything like it. The vicar, dressed in his nightclothes, was hanging from one of the bell ropes, his body still swinging slightly in the air, though obviously no longer enough to set the bell ringing. Of course, we cut him down as quickly as we could, desperately hoping that he might still be alive, but it was soon clear to me that the vicar was dead.

"It was then that I noticed the curate, Ronald Soames. He had just arrived and was standing at the back of the group of people in the tower doorway, so I told him to get all of the people out of the church and ordered Harry to make sure that no one should enter the bell tower until you arrived."

"The vicar's suicide is very distressing Constable Poole," Thorne said as our carriage slowed to a walk, "but I do not see why you need me."

"But don't you see, Rev. Thorne," Poole replied. "The only door to the bell tower was bolted from the inside, and there are no windows in the tower large enough for a man to climb through even if any of them opened, which they do not."

"Then clearly the vicar bolted the door before he took his own life," I explained patiently and perhaps a little patronizingly, "a perfectly natural precaution against being interrupted."

"Oh, he cannot have done that, Mr. Knowles," Constable Poole said in a very definite tone. "Oh no, that's not at all possible, for you see, the vicar's body was no longer warm when I cut him down. I am a policeman not a doctor or a detective, Mr. Knowles, but I saw death all too often in the Army during the Second Boer War, and even I know that the vicar was dead before someone tied him to that bell-rope this morning. It was murder, Rev. Thorne, and that's why I am out of my depth. The vicar's dead body was left hanging from a rope in a room secured from the inside, and that's just not possible, sir."

By the time Constable Poole had completed his story, thatched, whitewashed cottages began to appear on each side of the road, and we had soon reached the main street of Upper Sanditon village. I could see a small number of people milling around in the churchyard. At the main door stood a young man who I guessed from Poole's account to be the curate since he appeared to be rather officiously keeping bystanders well away from the entrance to the church.

As we approached the church door, the curate, who was clearly on familiar terms with my friend, stepped forward to greet us. He was a young man of medium height, in his mid-twenties and dressed in a clerical smock. As he walked towards Thorne, he held wide his arms as though to express the immensity of the shock which he felt.

"Terrible business, Rev. Thorne," Ronald Soames began. "I have done exactly as Constable Poole requested. No one has entered the church since the vicar's body was discovered, except for Harry Bailey who is keeping his eye on the doorway to the tower, so everything's secure for your investigation. It was I who suggested to Poole that he should involve you. I thought it to be wise. We need a man with your experience in such a delicate matter - the scandal, you know, will be terrible."

Rev. Thorne introduced me to the young man, and then the three of us walked past him into the church.

"If there is any way in which I can assist you, Rev. Thorne," called Soames as Constable Poole was leading us into the church, "do not hesitate to let me know!"

The interior of the church was dark, as is invariably the case with Norman churches. The bright early morning sunlight beat against the small east windows of the nave but was largely repulsed by their thick stained glass. In the gloom beyond the font, I detected Harry Bailey standing before the entrance to the bell tower guarding the opening where the door should have been; the unhinged door itself lay on its side to the right of the opening.

"You have seen nothing Harry? No one has come in or out?" Constable Poole enquired.

"No one, sir. Ah, Rev. Thorne, I am glad to see you, sir. Nothing has been touched since the body was taken down. It is still in there. We laid it on a bench and covered it with the altar cloth. Other than that, no one has touched anything, I can vouch for that. And now, Constable, if you have no more use for me, I must open up my business for the day. Horses will still want shoeing today, I suppose."

"Of course. Thank you for all that you have done, Harry," Poole replied, and then turning to Thorne continued, "I shall wait here and leave you to examine the room, Rev. Thorne. I have no doubt that you will also want to look at the body. When you have finished, I will make arrangements to have it removed."

Left alone, Rev. Thorne took a powerful magnifying lens from his pocket and fell to a minute examination of the room. Drawing on my experience as a hospital chaplain in France during The Great War, I looked closely at the body of the dead man. There was some sign of abrasion where the rope had cut into the neck, but neither bruising nor bleeding was present; this immediately confirmed to me that Constable Poole had been correct in his assertion that the vicar had been dead before the rope had been placed around his neck to make it appear as though he had hanged himself. In addition, I found that the limbs of the corpse were stiffening and becoming difficult to move, clearly the early stages of rigor mortis which, in humans, commences about three or four hours after death. Since it was now 7.55 a.m. by my pocket watch, this placed the vicar's death up to two hours before the ringing of the bells.

I replaced the altar cloth over the vicar's body and waited for Thorne to conclude his examination knowing much better than to interrupt him. It was some twenty minutes before he rather ostentatiously replaced the lens in his jacket and approached me.

"Well, Knowles, what does the body have to tell you?" he asked.

I reported my findings and asked in turn what his own investigation had produced.

"Very much as the admirable Constable Poole reported, my dear friend," Thorne replied. "These small, heavily leaded windows do not open; there is no possible exit other than the heavy door which Mr. Bailey was forced to entirely remove because it was locked from the inside. Yet this man, you assure me," Thorne gestured towards the body, "was undoubtedly murdered."

"But, Thorne," I exclaimed, "that is, as Poole says, simply not possible. Logically, there are only two explanations: either there was no murderer, which is the conclusion to which the staged suicide was supposed to mislead the police; or the murderer is still in the tower, which he clearly is not!"

"Really, my dear Knowles, you do still have a tendency to overly complicate matters, not to mention your weakness for the melodramatic. There is a third, perfectly adequate explanation which fits all of the facts and which, moreover, suggests the guilty party. I draw your attention to the tall cupboard beside the entrance."

I looked at the ancient cupboard, which was certainly tall enough to contain a man, but I immediately rejected this idea when I found that it was divided into narrow shelves, most of which were empty, so that no human body (except that perhaps of a child) could possible fit into it. I pointed this out to Thorne, who simply replied:

"What I draw your attention to is the recent fine scratches on the stone floor at the base of the cupboard."

I was about to look more closely, when a deep groan escaped from the mouth of Rev. Thorne who slumped forward against the wall and fell to his knees clutching his chest. I saw at once that his face was contorted into a mask of pain and had turned ashy white, the obvious signs of a heart attack or stroke.

"The vicarage, Knowles," Thorne gasped.

I was somewhat surprised that my own efforts to lift the limp body of my friend proved unavailing.

"Call Soames!" Thorne exclaimed in a whisper just before he lost consciousness entirely.

The young curate came running at my call followed closely by Poole. When I told them that I wanted Thorne carried into the vicarage, Soames effortlessly scooped Thorne into his arms and carried him across the churchyard. He laid Thorne gently on a couch in the vicar's study, and at my urging Poole and the curate left me to attend to my friend. Fearing the worst, I began to open a bottle of smelling salts which it is my habit to carry.

"Quite unnecessary, my dear Knowles!" said Thorne rising from the couch. "Moreover, we do not have much time. I shall search the bureau whilst you look at everything on the writing table."

"What exactly am I looking for, Thorne?" I enquired hiding my amazement at his sudden recovery.

"Motive, Knowles, motive!" Thorne replied. "This was no random act of violence. Whoever killed the vicar had a reason, and the key must be in the vicar's papers. Let us hope that the murderer has not had time entirely to cover his tracks."

I went over to the table where the vicar's papers lay in some disorder. I thought at first that this was simply the result of the vicar's untidiness, but another reason soon dawned on me.

"Thorne!" I exclaimed. "Someone has been here before us. No man leaves his papers in this degree of disorder; they have been searched already. I fear that our murderer has anticipated us."

"Knowles, we shall make a detective of you yet," Thorne replied. "I had just reached the same conclusion. See how the last three pages of the vicar's journal have been removed so carefully that only a trained observer would detect their removal."

Rev. Thorne passed me the journal. I noted that the vicar had written in pencil, and that last entry was dated three days ago. Scanning the entries for the previous two weeks, I found only day-to-day trivia.

"It seems," I concluded dismally, "that the evidence has entirely disappeared."

"Perhaps not," replied Thorne, snatching the journal from my hands in a burst of excitement.

Thorne took a BB pencil from the desk and began lightly shading the first unused page of the journal. Since the vicar had written with a firm hand, the impressions of several pages began to appear superimposed on one another creating only a confusion of shadow images which resembled a photographic negative. However, as Rev. Thorne reached the bottom of the page the word "Bishop" and the letters "RS" were clearly decipherable followed by an exclamation mark.

"And now, how did our murderer gain access?" asked Thorne, speaking, as was his habit during any investigation, more to himself than to me, and moving towards the window which he examined with his glass.

"It is as I expected. The window lock has been has been forced open by a blade inserted from the outside between the two window frames. Note the shiny abrasion in the metal caused by the blade, Knowles. Now we have our man!" Thorne concluded in a cry of triumph though I must admit that, though I had understood that "our man" was Soames, I still had no idea how we "had" him.

The sound brought Constable Poole and curate Soames running back into the room.

"Rev. Thorne," Soames gasped, his face suddenly pale, "you appear to have made a remarkable recovery."

"Indeed, Soames, though you seem to take no pleasure in it. Constable Poole, you may arrest Mr. Soames upon suspicion of murder."

The Constable looked shocked and replied, "I am sure, Rev. Thorne, that your say-so is enough for me - you have a reputation after all. But I shall have to present reasonable cause to the magistrate, so I will need some explanation."

Rev. Thorne sat down upon the couch, stretched his hands behind his head, leaned back, and then continued with evident relish:

"I am forced to begin with pure speculation which to a former detective sergeant is most unsatisfactory. In recent weeks, I believe that our curate came to suspect that the vicar had discovered something which, had it become public knowledge, would have ended his career in the Church and perhaps ruined his reputation forever. I can think of no other explanation for the indubitable fact that at about 3.00 a.m. this morning, Mr. Soames entered this room through that window.

"Knowles, be so good as to indicate to Poole the manner of entry whilst I continue. I fancy that you will find that Soames owns a long-bladed knife which will fit the mark which Knowles has no doubt indicated. Soames lighted the lamp on the writing table and searched through the vicar's papers looking for anything which might confirm his suspicions, something which might incriminate him. You will see that he carefully removed pages from the vicar's journal – Knowles, if you could again show Poole the evidence. Those missing pages (which he destroyed) told him that the vicar had arranged a meeting with the bishop in two days at which Soames had no doubt that the vicar intended to expose him.

"At some point, the vicar, having heard a noise and suspecting a burglary, came into the room. There was an argument and perhaps a brief struggle, though a very one-sided affair to be sure, since Soames is a healthy young man and the vicar was rather frail. During this altercation, I rather think that the vicar suffered a heart attack. I doubt very much that Mr. Soames intended to kill the vicar or he would have given himself more time to eliminate incriminating evidence. As it was, he now had a dead body to dispose of, so quickly rearranging the room to hide any evidence of the struggle, he carried the vicar to the church tower - just as easily as he carried me *from* the church, gentlemen – locked the door from the inside, and a little before 6.30 a.m. tied the rope around the vicar's neck to make his death appear to be suicide and set the bells ringing."

"But surely you are forgetting the locked door, Rev. Thorne," Soames stated with a contemptuous sneer. "I suppose that having locked it, I simply vanished into thin air only to reappear from outside the tower after the body had been discovered."

"Not at all, Mr. Soames," replied my friend. "I believe that I remarked to my friend Knowles just before I was taken so suddenly ill that the more intriguing the mystery the more prosaic the solution often is. You remained hidden behind the cupboard which you only had to slide out from the wall just a few inches to give you access to the slight alcove behind. Once the door had been removed, and Poole and the few others with him had rushed towards the hanging man to cut him down, you emerged behind them in the doorway as though you had only just arrived. Everyone's attention was taken up with task of getting the vicar's body down. No one saw anything suspicious because no one was looking for anything suspicious."

"But, Rev. Thorne," objected Constable Poole, "it was Soames himself who insisted that I involve you in the investigation. Why would he do that if he was himself the murderer? Tell me that."

"Vanity," replied Rev. Thorne. "A vice of which, I believe, Knowles has on more than one occasion accused me, though I, of course, deny the allegation."

Ronald Soames' head fell onto his chest as Constable Poole took a tight grip of his arm.

Thorne rose from the couch.

"I fear, Constable, that I can throw no light on the nature of the complaints which the vicar was about to lay before the bishop concerning his curate," he admitted, "but I have no doubt that diligent police work will be sufficient to uncover it. In my experience, the motives for murder are frequently much less dramatic than the crime itself, and much less interesting – particularly to a retired investigator such as myself. I suggest that you look into the church accounts. Good day!"

By the time we emerged from the vicarage, the sun had passed its zenith.

"And now, Knowles," Thorne said, "you appreciate the true dullness of my retirement in Upper Sanditon! I think that, since I recall you to have been cheated of your breakfast this morning, we should repair to the local hostelry where they serve an excellent lunch, and after that I have a particularly problematic orchid in the glasshouse upon which I should value your opinion."

Thus concluded what I believe to have been the final case in which my friend, The Rev Lyle Thorne, was involved, and thus truly began the many years of his retirement and his considerable contribution to the development of orchid cultivation.

A Chronology

March 1889 - Detective Sergeant Lyle Thorne resigns from the Metropolitan Police

1907 -   Rev. Lyle Thorne becomes Vicar of Sanditon

January 1910 -   Reginald Knowles becomes Thorne's curate

September 1911 - The Case of the Fallen Woman

April 1912 -   The Case of the Anonymous Cleric

May 1913 -   The Case of the Italian Bride

August 1913 -   The Case of the Missing Betrothed

November 1914 - Reginald Knowles ordained Army Chaplain

Spring 1927 -   Rev. Thorne retires to Upper Sanditon

August 1927 -   The Case of the Hanging Man

1948 -   Reverend Lyle Thorne dies and is buried in the churchyard at Upper Sanditon

About the Author

Ray Moore was born in Nottingham, England in 1950. He obtained his Master's Degree in Literature at Lancaster University in 1974 and then taught in secondary education for twenty-eight years before relocating to Florida with his wife in 2002. There he taught English and Information Technology in the International Baccalaureate program at Vanguard High School in Ocala.

He is now a full-time writer and fitness fanatic.

Also by Ray Moore

Fiction:

Further Investigations of The Reverend Lyle Thorne (published March 2013)

Non-fiction:

"The Stranger" by Albert Camus: A Critical Introduction (published October 2012)

"The General Prologue" by Geoffrey Chaucer: A Critical Introduction (published January 2013)

"Pride and Prejudice" by Jane Austen: A Critical Introduction (published July 2013)

Contact Information:

Email: moore.ray1@yahoo.com

12048721R00065

Printed in Great Britain
by Amazon.co.uk, Ltd.,
Marston Gate.